It would not be proper for a lady like Elise to fall in love with a simple cowboy, but...

"Say, I've got to go into town tomorrow for a few supplies. Why don't you ride in with me? We can talk then."

Elise threw her arms around his neck with enthusiastic abandon and hugged him tightly. "It sounds wonderful. I can't wait." She suddenly realized what she was doing and quickly withdrew her arms. She cleared her throat self-consciously and stood up, walking over to the porch railing. "The sky is so lovely in Texas," she said in an obvious attempt to change the subject. "I don't think I've ever seen so many stars."

Tanner strode over to join her. "It's a beautiful, clear night."

Elise sighed wistfully. "It's so peaceful and lovely here. Heavenly, don't you think?"

Tanner ignored the sky, choosing instead to move closer, concentrating his full attention on her upturned face. The light from inside the house cast a golden glow on her delicate features. An errant breeze carried with it her sweet scent of flowers, and he was reminded of how soft her skin felt to his touch. "Definitely heavenly." His whispered words were almost a caress.

Elise startled at the proximity of his voice. She hadn't heard him move so close. She glanced hesitantly in his direction and their eyes met. Elise's heart hammered wildly within her chest as Tanner placed his hands on her shoulders, gently turning her toward him. He brushed a wispy strand of hair from her face. "Elise," he whispered huskily, "I. . ."

NANCY LAVO is a gifted author from the big state of Texas where she lives with her husband and three children. *Her Father's Love* is Nancy's first historical inspirational romance.

Other Books by Nancy Lavo

HEARTSONG PRESENTS
HP133—A Change of Heart

Her Father's Love

Nancy Lavo

Heartsong Presents

To Margaret Rhoades and Jane Orcutt:
whose friendship blesses and refreshes me
and
whose wise counsel keeps me on my toes.

A note from the Author:
*I love to hear from my readers! You may write to me at
the following address:* **Nancy Lavo
Author Relations
P.O. Box 719
Uhrichsville, OH 44683**

ISBN 1-55748-895-9

HER FATHER'S LOVE

Cover illustration by Brian Bowman.

PRINTED IN THE U.S.A.

one

Seth,

I will be brief. Yesterday, I received an offer of marriage on behalf of Elise from Mr. Percival Bennett, of the Boston Bennetts. Mr. Bennett is a solid, dependable gentleman of excellent family and, at twenty-two, Elise is certainly of marriageable age.

I consider it a good match and plan to accept his offer on her behalf.

Due to the increased expenses that I will undoubtedly incur in the upcoming months, I must insist on a significant increase in my monthly allowance.

Claudia

"Rosa!" Seth Garver stormed across the library and threw open the heavy paneled door with a crash. "Rosa!"

A honey-skinned woman emerged from the kitchen, calmly drying her hands in her apron.

"What are you shouting about?" She tossed her long braid over her shoulder. "You sure got yourself worked up—" she stopped in midsentence to study the expression on his reddened face. "*Señor* Garver, are you all right?"

"It's the old crab. She's done it again." Seth began to pace across the polished plank floor, his boots pounding an agitated rhythm. "But this time she's gone too far."

"Old crab?" Understanding dawned slowly across Rosa's face. "You must mean Claudia's at it again." Her concerned frown melted into a laugh. "What does she want this time? By the look on your face, it must be more money."

Seth stopped in midstride. His voice was a strangled whisper. "It's Elise. She's gonna marry off my Elise." He resumed his frantic pacing. "I've got to stop her."

Rosa stepped into his path, hands planted firmly on her hips. "What do you mean she's gonna marry off Elise?" she demanded. "What are you talking about?"

"This!" Seth shook the paper he clutched in his fist. "Some fella wants to marry Elise, and Claudia's going to let him." He paused briefly to scan the missive then read aloud, "Mr. Percival Bennett, . . .a solid, dependable gentleman." He glared at Rosa. "What kind of description is that? Sounds more like my mule than a suitor!" He waved the offending letter in the air. "And what kind of name is Percival, anyway? Sounds uppity, if you ask me."

"Never mind the name," Rosa snapped impatiently. "Can she do it, Seth? Can Claudia really do it?"

Seth said nothing as he ran trembling fingers through his salt-and-pepper hair. "I've got to get her home," he mumbled finally. "I've got to see her. Twenty-two years old. . .it's been too long." He sidestepped Rosa to pace more rapidly.

Rosa raised a skeptical brow. "*Señor* Garver, if I'm recalling correctly, Claudia said she'd never send Elise here." As an afterthought she added, "Unless you were dying, of course."

"Dying." Seth halted his pacing. "Dying?" he repeated. A hint of a smile touched his lips. "Dying! Now why didn't

I think of that?"

"*Señor* Garver," Rosa warned, alarmed by the glimmer she saw in his eyes. "You're as healthy as a horse; you and I both know that."

"But Claudia doesn't."

Rosa tried again. "*Señor*, I can see trouble in those eyes of yours. It's lying you're talking about. And lying's a sin."

Seth was grinning broadly now. "Desperate times call for desperate measures."

&

"Do you mind if I take this seat beside you?"

Elise looked up from her well-worn copy of *Mrs. Rhoade's Complete Handbook of Courteous Behavior and Social Graces for Young Women* and smiled politely at the ruddy-faced woman standing beside her. "Not at all. Please, sit down."

With a groan, the woman eased her bulky frame into the seat. "I always look for someone to talk to when I travel. Seems to make the time pass faster." She offered her chubby hand in greeting. "I'm Mrs. Mavis Teekle, from Fort Worth."

Elise hesitated for a split second, nibbling her lower lip with uncertainty. Aunt Claudia had been most insistent that she was not to speak to anyone while traveling, citing endless examples of the treachery that awaited unsuspecting women travelers.

She slanted a gaze toward her companion. The woman did not look dangerous and it had been such a long tedious trip. Perhaps one short conversation would not hurt anything.

Still, she vacillated. To defy Aunt Claudia would be unthinkable.

Her next thought settled the matter once and for all. Decorum. Hadn't Aunt Claudia drilled into her the importance of showing respect to elders by speaking when spoken to? Dangerous or not, Elise would converse with Mavis Teekle. After all, it was the proper thing to do.

With a warm smile, Elise accepted the older woman's hand. "How do you do. I'm Elise Garver, from Boston."

Mavis's small eyes opened wide. "I should have guessed," she clucked admiringly. "You city girls are always at the height of fashion, aren't you."

"Ma'am?"

"Just look at you. All gussied up in that pretty, pink-colored suit with a red blouse and a bright blue hat to match. Country folks like me would never have the sense to put them colors together."

Elise felt the blush creep across her face. "Actually—"

"From Boston you say?" Mavis interrupted. "That's a long way from home for a pretty, young woman like you. Now don't tell me; let me guess." She studied Elise momentarily. "I know. You've come to Texas to meet your betrothed. How exciting!" She clasped her hands together gleefully, obviously enraptured with the romantic notion.

Elise shook her head. "Oh, no ma'am, nothing like that. I'm on my way to Crossroads to meet my father."

"Oh." Disappointed with Elise's answer, Mavis slumped back against the seat.

"But it really is quite exciting," Elise insisted. She leaned toward the woman and added in a whisper, "You see, I haven't seen him since I was three years old."

"Mercy!" Mavis was on the edge of her seat once more, her attention riveted on Elise. "You haven't seen your own father since you were three?"

Elise nodded. "My mother died then, and my father sent me to Aunt Claudia's in Boston, that's my mother's only sister, to raise me. I've been there ever since."

Mavis laid a consoling hand on Elise's arm. "Poor man. Must have been out of his head with grief to send his little girl away."

Elise smiled brightly and nodded. "You know, that's exactly what I've always thought." Her smile faded slightly. "Aunt Claudia said it was because he didn't want me." Elise's tone was matter-of-fact as she continued, "She says my father is a barbarian who killed my mother then shipped me off, like an orphan."

She did not miss the shocked look on her companion's face and was quick to add, "Oh, Mrs. Teekle, he didn't kill her, of course. My mother died of the fever. But there weren't any doctors for her when she died. According to Aunt Claudia, that's as good as murdering her."

"You poor darlin'." Mavis's expression was tragic. "That's about the saddest thing I've ever heard. It must be so painful for you to think about it."

"To tell the truth, I'm used to it by now. I'll bet Aunt Claudia's told the story at least a hundred times. Do you know it's the all-time favorite topic at our Ladies Literary Society meetings? She's gotten so good at telling it now that by the time she's finished there's rarely a dry eye in the room." Elise flashed a wry smile. "My father is practically a legend."

Mavis was silent for a moment, trying to digest all she had heard. "Why don't you tell me about him, dear? Tell me about your father."

Elise warmed to the topic. "He's a wonderful man, Mrs. Teekle. Kind and gentle and very strong. The kind of father every girl dreams of." Her green eyes sparkled with enthusiasm. "He's handsome, too. Real tall, with broad shoulders and strong hands." Her voice grew more animated. "His skin is deeply tanned from all the time he spends in the sun . . .he's a cowboy, you see, and he has tiny little crinkles at the corners of his eyes when he smiles, which is almost all the time."

"I just can't imagine where your Aunt Claudia gets the idea that the man has abandoned you. It's obvious to me that you two have stayed in close contact over the years, with lots of letters and photographs, I'll bet."

"Well, no." Elise cleared her throat uncomfortably. "Not actually."

Mavis nodded her understanding. "Well, as busy as a cowboy's life is, he's probably doing the best he can, just getting a letter or two off to you each year."

"There haven't been any letters, Mrs. Teekle." Elise felt the warm color stain her cheeks.

"None at all?" Mavis's voice rose to an astonished squeak. She seemed to note Elise's discomfort and added quickly, "Aw honey, that's nothing to be ashamed of. There's lots of cowboys that can't write. Running cattle doesn't leave much time for schooling. Besides, just a photograph can tell you plenty about a person."

"I've never seen a single photograph of my father." Mavis had to strain to hear Elise's whispered confession. "Aunt Claudia forbade me to even mention his name."

"But the way you described him. . . ."

Elise raised an earnest gaze to her companion. "I hope

you don't think I've misled you. It sounds odd I suppose, but I don't need a photograph of him to know what he looks like." She studied her hands resting in her lap. "I've dreamed of him so often, I have a very clear picture of him in my heart."

For the first time in her life, Mavis found herself speechless. When at long last her voice returned, she asked softly, "Child, after all this time, why are you going to him now?"

"He's dying," Elise replied with renewed cheerfulness. "At least, that's what the doctor says." She turned a dazzling smile to Mrs. Teekle. "Isn't it nice to know they've got a doctor in Crossroads now?"

Mavis's mouth dropped open in surprise. She tried to speak, but could only sputter.

Elise saw her concern. "Oh, he won't really die. Don't you see? All these years, I've been hoping my father would want me to come home. This is it. His doctor sent me a letter, saying Father was dying and asking me to come to Texas." Her voice faded to a whisper and tears glittered in her eyes. "He wants me to come home." She cleared her throat self-consciously. "Once we're together, I'm sure he'll be fine. Good as new."

Mavis opened her mouth to reply, then seemed to think the better of it. Instead, she shook her head and turned to stare out the window across the aisle.

Elise caught the look of disbelief on Mavis's face as she turned away. It was obvious she did not share Elise's optimism. An embarrassed flush warmed her face as she realized she'd practically talked the woman's ear off. She wasn't certain why she had poured out her heart like that. Must be nerves.

Thankfully Aunt Claudia had not been here to witness her appalling lack of restraint. This was just the sort of behavior that had earned Elise many a stern lecture over the years on the merits of propriety.

"Don't be such a magpie," Aunt Claudia would say. "Gentle women of breeding do not run on so. It's that bad blood of your father's showing through. Heaven knows what a trial it is for me to try to make something of you."

Elise brushed the unpleasant memory aside as she checked the timepiece attached to her bodice for the umpteenth time. According to her calculations, she had another hour before she would reach the station. She sighed impatiently and settled back into her seat to study the rugged Texas landscape through the soot-streaked window.

Texas. Elise could not believe she was actually seeing Texas again. It was lovely, she mused. Everything looked green and alive. Not at all what she expected. She'd been so young when she left the last time, too young to remember the endless, flat, wide open spaces or the life she had had there with her father.

Her heart soared. Her father. She had to pinch herself as a reminder that it was not a dream. She was finally going to be with him. Excitement bubbled up within her.

Ever since she'd been a young child, her father had been foremost in her mind. Over the years, she had spent countless hours comforting herself with thoughts of him. It was her father who whispered endearments to her when she felt the sting of Aunt Claudia's sharp tongue. He was the one by her side when she faced the terrors of a lonely dark night. His was the willing ear with which she shared her innermost secrets.

Until today, Elise never mentioned these dreams to anyone. Aunt Claudia was not interested in what she termed "the fanciful products of Elise's overactive imagination." In fact, she had forbidden her to mention his name. Elise couldn't hold it against her. After all, Aunt Claudia had been terribly hurt when her sister had died and, in her frustration, she blamed the only person she could—Seth Garver. But Elise didn't blame him. She loved him and she knew he loved her.

There was one wrinkle in her perfect dream: father and daughter were separated. Elise had struggled long with the matter of why her father had never sent for her. After all, a man who loved his daughter like her father loved her would most certainly want her by his side. Yet she had never heard from him, not once in all those years.

Elise was eleven or twelve years old when the answer had finally dawned on her. She had been reading the story of a family separated through poverty when she found a plausible explanation. The father and mother went to a workhouse and the children were sent to an orphanage.

Her father was poor. That explained everything perfectly. Seth Garver must be poor, so poor that he did not want to bring his daughter to Texas until he could afford to take care of her. He was a proud man, of that she was certain. After all, he was a Texan and she knew from reading any book she could find about the state, that Texans, especially cowboys, were very proud.

With that discovery, the nagging question was settled once and for all in Elise's mind. And it stirred within her a deep desire to help her father in any way she could.

The recent letter saying her father wanted to see her was

the long-awaited culmination of all her dreams. True, there was the matter of his dying, but Elise did not take it too seriously. God would not go to all the trouble to get them together, just to tear them apart.

The conductor stepped into the car. "Crossroads. Next stop, Crossroads." Elise checked her timepiece again. The train was right on time.

Mavis pressed a crumpled piece of paper into Elise's hand. "Honey, this is my name and address. I'd like you to have it, just in case you need me."

Elise smiled politely at Mrs. Teekle's kindness and tucked the paper into her reticule. It was obvious the woman thought she was making a mistake. Elise couldn't blame her; she knew the evidence leaned heavily against her dreams. She, too, struggled with doubts. But even then, deep in her heart, she knew her father loved her.

When the train finally screeched to a noisy stop, Elise stepped quickly over Mavis and her bags. In her excitement, she was halfway down the aisle before she remembered her manners. She turned and waved. "Good-bye Mrs. Teekle. It was a pleasure meeting you." Etiquette satisfied, she turned and ran.

She paused momentarily on the top step of the train to breathe deeply of the warm spring air. Happiness surged through her. She was here at long last. Texas. Home.

Elise descended lightly to the planked platform to survey the tiny station. Two rough benches, both empty, leaned against the wall. There was none of the customary hustle and bustle one usually found at a depot. In fact, the place appeared deserted.

She caught her lower lip in her teeth as a tiny doubt

nibbled at her confidence. Could her father have forgotten she was coming?

The dire warning that Aunt Claudia had delivered just days ago as they stood waiting for the train in Boston, rang in her ears. "I can't very well forbid you to go." She had raised her chin a notch as she addressed Elise in her haughtiest tone. "It's my Christian duty to fulfill a dying man's request. But," her steely eyes grew hard as she continued, "mark my words, you're making a mistake. The man's a barbarian. He's not interested in you, Elise. Never has been."

Having delivered her cruelest barb, Aunt Claudia had folded her arms across her chest triumphantly, waiting for Elise to change her mind about the trip and stay home.

Elise had surprised them both by getting on the train.

Now she suffered a momentary qualm, one of many she had fought to suppress during the long trip. Had she misjudged him? Was her father truly a barbarian? After all, what did she really know about the man?

Nonsense, she reassured herself. Surely even a barbarian would know to send someone to the station to pick up his daughter. Anyway, it was too late for second thoughts. She was here now and she had come too far to lose heart.

She glanced over her shoulder to see Mavis's round face pressed against the window, worry etched in her plump features. Elise mustered a brave smile for her and waved before turning again to the vacant station.

She took a deep, fortifying breath. "It's going to be all right," she whispered aloud. She smoothed the jacket of her traveling suit, adjusted her bonnet, squared her slim shoulders, and marched resolutely into the station.

Once inside, she paused, blinking hard, waiting for her eyes to adjust from the bright sunlight to the darkened interior.

With the exception of the man seated behind the ticket window on the far side of the room, the station appeared to be deserted as well. Elise ignored the niggling fear tormenting her and decided her first course of action should be to check with him. Perhaps he knew of her father.

She started toward him when a movement to her right caught her attention. A tall man wearing a dark cowboy hat emerged from the shadows.

"Your name Garver?" It was not a question, but rather an accusation.

"Yes, I'm Miss Garver." She hoped her voice didn't reflect the intimidation she felt as the cowboy loomed over her. She studied his face, her efforts hampered by the poor lighting. He had dark hair and a mustache, that much she could make out. And, judging from the harsh line of his mouth, he seemed to be angry with her. "Are . . .are you here to take me home?"

"I'm here to take you to Seth's place," he growled, placing extra emphasis on the word Seth.

It was obvious to Elise that she had gotten off on the wrong foot with the man, although she could not figure out why. She decided to start over. She took a tentative step toward him and extended a small, gloved hand. "I'm so glad to meet you. I'm Elise Garver."

The man simply glared. He pointedly ignored the outstretched hand, choosing instead to brush past her and stalk out of the station.

Elise stood immobilized, the smile still frozen on her face, an embarrassed flush creeping over her cheeks. She could not remember a time in all of her twenty-two years of ever being treated so rudely. In her sheltered existence in Boston, even sworn enemies hated one another with propriety and decorum.

Her slight shoulders sagged with disappointment. The meeting was nothing of the warm homecoming she had envisioned. The doubts that had plagued her across the country crowded in. Perhaps she had made a mistake, after all.

A sudden thought brought a genuine smile to her lips. The man was obviously a cowboy, that much she could surmise from his attire. According to Aunt Claudia, cowboys were uneducated barbarians. Elise's smile grew wide. He hadn't intended to slight her, he simply had not known any better.

Her heart went out to him immediately. Poor man. No wonder he was so cross. She knew firsthand how painful it could be to be socially inept. Maybe she could help him. Perhaps during the course of her stay, she could teach him some basic etiquette.

Endlessly relieved, she followed him outside to a wagon where he was loading her trunks. A huge black dog of questionable parentage yapped excitedly from his perch on the wagon bench. Maybe she'd have better luck with the dog.

"Hello there, fella." Elise reached up to pat the dog's shaggy head. "What's your name?"

"*Her* name's Becky." The cowboy's mocking voice was low and velvety smooth.

Elise gasped. She hadn't heard him come up behind

her. Before she could turn around to respond, two large hands grasped her around the waist and carelessly tossed her up onto the wooden bench.

"Ooof!" She landed with a surprised thud. Her emerald green eyes flashed as she whirled around to enlighten him of her opinion of being manhandled. cowboy or not, his behavior was highly improper.

Elise hadn't fully recovered when the wagon dipped slightly as he took his place on the bench beside her. For a big man, he certainly moved quietly.

She faced him, ready to begin his education with a lesson as to the proper way to assist a lady, when she noticed the expression in his dark eyes. The cold challenge she found there silenced her complaint. The cowboy looked positively ferocious. She didn't doubt that with the slightest provocation, he'd leave her there stranded.

Never mind the lesson, she thought, smoothing her skirts. *It wasn't worth it. cowboys probably had few dealings with ladies, anyway. My father won't be like that,* she reassured herself. *He will be gentle and polite.*

Her father. Elise relaxed visibly at the thought. Her trip was almost complete. In no time at all she'd be reunited with her father. Her pulse began to race. It wasn't a dream. Seth Garver had asked her to come to Texas. He loved her, just as she had always imagined.

"I can't wait to see my father," Elise voiced her thoughts aloud.

"You don't sound too worried about him. I mean the fact that Doc Kalina says he's dyin'." The cowboy's voice was hard.

"I'm not," she replied brightly. She wouldn't try to

explain to the irritable cowboy that she knew beyond a shadow of a doubt that her father would be all right. She remembered too clearly the look Mavis Teekle had given her when she had tried to explain it to her.

Elise heard his sharp intake of breath at her reply, but she refused to meet the piercing eyes that burned into her. She couldn't expect him to understand.

"What a lovely town," Elise said as she studied the graying, wooden buildings lining the dirt street. A few people, mostly men, strolled the planked sidewalks. While it lacked the sophistication of New England, Elise found it charming and exciting.

She longed to ask questions about the town and its inhabitants but, with a quick glance toward the stony countenance of her formidable escort, she elected to wait and ask her father.

The wagon rattled through the center of Crossroads, then set a course due west. Wide open stretches of land flanked the well-traveled dirt road. Elise studied the gently rolling landscape with interest. It was so unlike Boston.

Unfettered by civilization, it seemed to promise freedom and opportunity. She began to understand the strange draw that the West offered. Here there was the chance to begin again.

Overhead, the sky was a sweeping canopy of clearest blue. A warm breeze danced across the land, carrying with it the sweet scent of spring. The swaying vegetation was bright green with the advent of a new season. Scrubby trees and cactus dotted the grassy fields.

The warmth of the late afternoon sun and the rhythmic

rocking of the wagon had a sedating effect on Elise. With Becky wedged between herself and the cowboy to provide a buffer, the two rode in silence.

Elise studied the primitive shanties, built of mud or wood, that were scattered randomly across the open terrain. Each time the wagon came within view of one, she held her breath in anticipation. Any one of these could house her beloved father.

A smile stole across her lips. She knew his home would be crude, not the luxurious surroundings she had shared with Aunt Claudia in Boston, but that didn't matter. They would be together. She would be there for him, to nurse him back to health. That had been her fondest dream. To be useful to him. To provide for him. To be wanted by him.

Gradually the landscape changed. The once-open fields on either side of the road were now enclosed with endless stretches of barbed wire fence. When half an hour had passed since Elise had last sighted a house, her patience waned. "How much longer?" Her question broke the long silence.

The cowboy's eyes never left the road. "This is Garver land now. We ought to be at the house in a few minutes." His deep voice was expressionless.

Elise roused from her comfortable lethargy at the mention of Garver land. She sat up ramrod straight on the bench, giving him her full attention. "I beg your pardon, I'm afraid I don't understand."

The cowboy turned to face her, his dark hat pulled low over his brow. He spoke slowly, enunciating each word as though addressing a small child. "We passed the Garver marker a while back. Won't be long till we can see the main house."

For a moment, Elise was still, her mind racing as she tried to digest the information. This was Garver land? How could a poor man own so much land? There had to be a mistake.

The cowboy's deep voice pierced the silence. "There's the house now." He pointed to the horizon.

Suddenly, she didn't want to see. The sight of the house might confirm the gnawing fear growing inside her. She didn't want to know. The cowboy kept his hand extended, waiting for her to respond. Elise forced herself to look.

It was a large, white, two-story structure with a long porch stretching across the front, an impressive home even by Boston standards. Several smaller buildings and enclosures were scattered beside it.

Elise tore her eyes away, a stricken look on her face. "There's got to be a mistake," she said weakly. She reached a tentative hand to rest on his arm. Imploring green eyes met steely dark ones. "This is some kind of mistake. I am looking for Seth Garver."

"No mistake."

"How long. . . ?" The tortured whisper caught in her throat. "How long has he lived here?"

"Long time." The cowboy's dark eyes held hers. "Is there a problem?" There was no kindness in his voice.

No sound would come from her throat. She shook her head mutely as she drew her hand back to her lap. There was no problem at all. She had all the facts. It was just that the facts did not line up with her long-cherished dream.

Her father owned a huge home and all the land as far as the eye could see. He wasn't poor, too poor to raise his only daughter. He was rich.

She'd been wrong. All those years, clutching tenaciously to the hope that he would send for her as soon as he could, believing doggedly in his devotion and love, she'd been terribly wrong.

"Why? Why did he wait to send for me now?"

The cowboy seemed impatient with her. "Isn't it obvious? The man is dying. He's trying to tie up loose ends."

"Loose ends," she repeated mindlessly.

Suddenly, Elise felt hollow inside, completely void of any emotion. Her beautiful dream had died.

two

A slight woman in a bright red dress and white apron stood on the porch, waving frantically as the cowboy maneuvered the wagon around to the front of the house.

"*Hola*!" The woman shouted. "Welcome!"

Elise sat atop the wagon bench, unmoving. Her usually quick mind felt sluggish, her though processes dulled. The joyful anticipation of meeting her father had evaporated, leaving her limp.

The cowboy appeared noiselessly at her side to help her down from the wagon. Elise offered no protest. Again, large hands encompassed her waist as he lowered her to the ground. He was gentler this time, probably for the benefit of the woman on the porch, Elise thought wryly. Not that it mattered to Elise. Nothing mattered now.

Face to face, she took the opportunity to study him at close range. The cowboy was younger than she had thought, surely no more than thirty years old, and handsome. Her eyes widened as her heart gave an uncharacteristic flutter. Really handsome. With his hat pulled down so far on his face, she hadn't noticed his strong, ruggedly chiseled features or dark wavy hair.

Their eyes met briefly. His were dark, she noted, almost black. His expression was grim as he released her.

"You're here! You're here!" The strange woman from the porch pounced upon her, first hugging Elise to her chest, then drawing her back to study her face, finally pulling her back into an enthusiastic embrace. "We've waited so long to see you."

"Thank you," Elise's reply was somewhat muffled because her face remained compressed against the woman's shoulder. She was completely rattled. No one in Boston had ever hugged her like that. In truth, no one had ever hugged her at all. This open display of affection was so foreign to Elise, she had no idea as to the proper response.

Elise's entire life had been dictated by the strict adherence to *Mrs. Rhoades's Complete Handbook of Courteous Behavior and Social Graces for Young Women* and, as she racked her brain, she was quite certain that nowhere in the handbook was it explained how one greeted affectionate strangers. So what should she do now?

Mrs. Rhoades often advocated taking a deep breath to clear one's head. Perhaps with some air, something would come to her. Two deep breaths later, Elise was still uninspired. Not wishing to commit a social blunder, Elise gently disengaged herself and extended her hand in the formal greeting to which she was accustomed. "I'm Elise Garver."

Rosa smiled warmly. "*Sí*, of course you are. I can see it in those green eyes. You've got your father's eyes, you do."

At the mention of her father, Elise self-consciously dropped her gaze to the floor, the corner of her lower lip caught between her teeth.

"I've forgotten my manners. I am Rosa Viegas, your father's housekeeper." She offered a broad, white smile, a striking contrast to her golden skin. "Speaking of which, I am certain he is anxious to see you. Come, I'll lead you to him."

Elise followed obediently in Rosa's wake, dread weighing down her slender limbs. She briefly considered delaying the encounter by pleading exhaustion, but thought better of it. It would not be correct to keep her father waiting.

She stole a quick look around as they stepped inside. It was a lovely home, tastefully appointed with handsome furnishings. She found no pleasure in that fact. A mud hut would have suited her just fine. The obvious wealth displayed in her father's home served only to remind Elise of the foolishness of her dream. A lost dream.

The women climbed a long flight of stairs, walked to the end of the hall, and paused before a polished oak door. Rosa knocked softly.

"Come in."

Elise's knees felt weak and her stomach churned. At last, the moment she had been waiting for—the realization of her life's dreams. But with the information now in her possession, she was not at all certain how she would react to the man inside. He was a complete stranger to her now. And she was a "loose end."

Rosa swung the door open and stepped aside for Elise to pass. Heavy draperies at the windows blocked the afternoon sun, bathing the room in shadows. Elise took several hesitant steps toward the bed. Propped up against a wall of pillows was a huge man with an unruly crop of dark hair threaded with silver.

They studied each other in silence.

"Elise. It's really you." His voice faltered. "Come closer and let me see you."

Elise stepped closer to the bed, her hands clasped tightly before her. Her heart beat wildly in her chest. This was surely her father. She'd have known him anywhere.

He looked just as she imagined he would, ruggedly hand-some with warm, compassionate eyes. She was relieved to see that his illness had not yet sapped the vitality from him.

Face to face with the man of her dreams, a tiny spark of hope ignited within her. Maybe the cowboy was wrong. Maybe she was more than a "loose end" to her father.

She moved to the side of his bed, pulse pounding in her ears, waiting to hear him declare how much he loved her and had missed her. And how much he had wanted her home.

He simply stared. An awkward silence stretched be-tween them. Elise could hear the ticking of a clock.

"You are lovely," Seth whispered finally. "How proud your mother would be to see you now."

The polite compliment was a far cry from the pledge of love she longed to hear. It only seemed to confirm what the cowboy had spoken. Elise felt as though her heart would break. "Thank you, sir," she responded stiffly as she tried to mask her disappointment. "Aunt Claudia did her best."

"Claudia!" her father barked. "That woman's never done a good thing in her life."

Elise's wide eyes reflected her astonishment at his out-burst. "Sir?"

He was silenced from further comment by Rosa who began to fluff his pillows vigorously while pinning him with a censorious stare. "It's nothing, dear." Rosa smiled soothingly at Elise, then turned her gaze back to Seth. "Your father's thinking has been somewhat clouded by his *illness*." She placed special emphasis on the last word.

"I'm sorry. I was distressed to hear of your illness, sir."

Actually, Elise had been delighted when she received his letter saying he was dying and wished to see her.

She never believed he would die. She thought the sickness would signal a beginning for their lives together as father and daughter. How could she have been so wrong?

A sharp rap at the door caught her attention. She was surprised to see the cowboy stride across the room and stand on the opposite side of her father's bed. "I'm sorry, Seth. I needed to talk to you. Trouble with some of the fences. Am I interrupting anything?" He fixed Elise with a dark stare.

"Tanner, my boy, I guess you've had the chance to meet my daughter, Elise."

"We—" Elise began.

"Yes. We've met." Tanner's curt reply cut her off.

Elise cleared her throat in acute embarrassment. "I fear I've detained you long enough, sir. I'll leave you two alone to your discussion." She turned and left the room with all the dignity she could muster. Was there no end to the rudeness of that cowboy?

Rosa appeared at her side. "I'll bet you're tired after all your traveling. Let's get you settled in your room. You can freshen up and take a nice nap before supper."

She guided Elise to a room at the top of the stairs, down the hall from her father's. "Do you like it?" she asked anxiously.

Elise nodded her approval. "It's lovely." The room had obviously been decorated with a woman in mind. An elegant paper of trailing green vines blooming with pale pink roses covered the walls. Delicate lace curtains hung in the windows. The large bed heaped with soft coverlets looked especially inviting.

Rosa kept up a steady stream of comforting chatter while she bustled through the room. "I see Tanner has brought your trunks up. I'll put your things away later. Why don't you lie down and try to rest for a while. Traveling can be so tiring."

Elise sat at the dressing table and took the pins from her hair. With the silver brush she'd carried in her valise, she began to work through the tangled waves.

Rosa paused behind her. "What beautiful hair you have. Reminds me of my own daughter's." She addressed Elise's reflection in the mirror. "She used to love it when I brushed it for her. Do you mind?" Rosa gestured for Elise to hand her the brush.

Again Elise was startled by the easy, affectionate manner of Rosa. She was even more surprised to find she liked it. With a shy smile, she relinquished the brush to Rosa . "No one's brushed my hair for me since I was a little girl. Aunt Claudia said I could do it myself."

At the grunt of disapproval from Rosa, she added, "I hope I haven't made her sound callous. It's nothing like that. It's just that Aunt Claudia was always very careful not to spoil me with too much affection."

Rosa chose to keep her opinion of Aunt Claudia to herself as she continued to brush Elise's thick, mahogany tresses with gentle strokes. "It's nice to have someone here to look after. My daughter got married last year. She and her husband have gone to El Paso to start a ranch." Tears filled Rosa's eyes. "It was so hard to let her go. El Paso's so far away."

Elise felt Rosa's sorrow keenly. She knew how hard it was

to be alone. With unaccustomed boldness, she laid a comforting hand on Rosa's hand that rested on her shoulder.

Rosa smiled as she brushed away an errant tear. "You'll have to forgive the ramblings of an old woman." She stopped brushing to meet Elise's gaze. "I guess in my own way I'm telling you that if you ever need someone, you know, someone to talk to, well, I'm an experienced mother who's looking for someone to take care of."

"Thank you, Rosa." Tears glistened in her eyes as she whispered, "Your daughter is a very lucky woman."

Rosa paused from her brushing. "You know—" she stopped in mid sentence and laid the brush on the dressing table. "Never mind. We'll have plenty of time to talk later, but for now, I think a nap would be best."

Elise slipped out of her traveling suit and burrowed gratefully between the crisp sheets that smelled of spring and sunshine. She hadn't realized how truly tired she was.

"Rest now, little one." Rosa pulled the covers up over Elise's shoulders then bent and kissed her forehead before slipping noiselessly from the room.

ﾞa

Several hours later, Rosa peeked in to study the still slumbering form. She intended to call Elise to dinner, but it was obvious that what the exhausted young woman needed most was rest. . .and lots of love.

Rosa shook her head in frustration as she pulled the door closed behind her. It was inconceivable that a child could be raised without tenderness. In her own demonstrative family, hugs and kisses were a big part of every day.

Yet, she knew after meeting Elise that afternoon, the young

woman had received neither. Rosa vowed to God she wouldn't let her go until she'd gotten all the love she had missed.

≈

Tanner pounded his pillow viciously before dropping back against it to stare at the ceiling. His temper was still boiling, and he knew it would be a long time till he found sleep.

"Conniving, scheming little brat. Never in my life have I ever seen a bolder woman than our little Miss Garver." He rolled over onto his side, his head propped against his hand. "You should have seen her, Becky, arriving here just as fancy as you please. She might think she's fooling us with those slick city ways, but I've got her figured out real good."

Becky moved to the rug beside his bed and whimpered softly.

"Sure, she's pretty. I'm not blind. But trust me, Becky, behind those great big green eyes and pretty smile is a greedy woman."

She whimpered again, this time scratching lightly on the bed.

Tanner's large hand dropped down to scratch her behind the ears. "Yeah, she did smell real sweet, didn't she." He smiled briefly at the memory of lifting her from the wagon, his hands easily spanning her tiny waist. She smelled heavenly to him, like a whole field of flowers. He could almost smell her now.

His smile disappeared abruptly. "That doesn't change anything. Elise Garver is trouble, and the sooner we send her packin' to Boston, the better."

three

The tantalizing aroma of coffee wafted under Elise's nose, causing her to stir slightly. *No need to hurry,* she told herself, *Aunt Claudia won't be up until noon.* She burrowed more deeply into the covers.

The coffee was relentless in its assault. Elise's eyes flickered open reluctantly. For a moment, she was confused. Where was she?

Bright sunlight filtered through the lace-covered windows, bathing her face in its warmth. Elise sat up with a start. "This isn't Boston. This is home!" Initially crushed by yesterday's disappointing meeting with her father, the new day brought with it new hope. She was out of the bed in a flash.

She found to her surprise that her trunks were empty and her clothes were already hung in the wardrobe, everything neatly pressed. *Rosa,* Elise thought with a smile. She studied the garments carefully, finally selecting a day dress of emerald silk. She wanted to look just right for her father. If only she could remember what color of shoes to wear.

Suppose Tanner's right, Elise thought as she buttoned up her dress. *Suppose my father's only interest in me is to tie up loose ends. Should I give up now?* She shook her head *Of course not. I'm not giving up the one chance I have for a real father.* She chewed her lip thoughtfully. *I just can't.*

So my only option is to change his mind.

As she sat at the dressing table, putting the finishing touches on her hair, Elise continued to ponder the situation. She needed a plan of action; one in which she could earn her father's love. She balked slightly at the thought. It seemed a bit improper, scheming to win his affection. She doubted that either Aunt Claudia or Mrs. Rhoades would approve, but she could see no other alternative. She shrugged at her reflection. Desperate times called for desperate measures.

Elise followed the fragrant path of coffee to the kitchen where she found Rosa and Tanner seated at the table. "Good morning," she called from the doorway as she paused to scratch Becky behind the ears. "Do you mind if I join you?"

"You're up. *Bueno*, good." Rosa was on her feet instantly. "Come sit down, let me get you a cup of coffee and some breakfast. You must be starving."

"Famished. Thank you, Rosa." Elise smiled hesitantly at Tanner as she took the seat across the table from him. He said nothing as his dark gaze raked over her.

Rosa placed a cup of coffee and a filled plate in front of Elise. "I'm sorry you didn't get dinner last night. I came up to wake you, but you were sleeping so soundly, I hated to disturb you."

Elise flashed her a grateful smile before taking a long draught from her cup. "I was more tired than I realized. It was kind of you to let me sleep." She laid her cup on the table. "And thank you so much for pressing all my things and putting them away."

"It was my pleasure. It's wonderful to have a woman to

look after." Rosa's dark eyes glowed. "And didn't I have fun looking at all your fancy dresses. I've gotta say, you've got the finest clothes I've ever laid eyes on. Such pretty colors."

"Too *many* colors," Elise muttered under her breath. Belatedly remembering her manners, she added, "Thank you. They are lovely, aren't they. Aunt Claudia has always been quite emphatic about the importance of correct attire. She's spent a fortune on them, I'm afraid."

Tanner gave a snort of disgust and rose to his feet. "Thanks for breakfast, Rosa."

"You're not leaving, are you? I was hoping you could show Elise around the place this morning."

Tanner scooped his hat off the table and dropped it onto his head. "Sorry, Rosa." He patted her shoulder affectionately. "Too busy." Without so much as a glance toward Elise, he disappeared through the door.

Rosa clucked disapprovingly. "Wonder what's got into the man?"

"It's me, I'm afraid," Elise confessed, "although I'm not quite certain what I've done."

Rosa patted her hand. "Nonsense. He's just got himself worked up about the fences, that's all."

"The fences?"

Rosa nodded, rising to her feet. "He and Seth are both worried. Thieving rustlers been cutting 'em." She began to clear away the empty plates.

Elise made a mental note to find out more about the fences. If they were of interest to her father, then she would be interested, too. Any common ground would help her earn a place in his heart.

"Rosa, when can I see my father?"

"He said he'd see you this afternoon." Rosa missed the look of disappointment on Elise's face. "He thought you would like to see the ranch this morning."

Elise chafed at the delay. Her time was so limited, she wanted to see her father so she could get started on her plan right away.

Rosa seemed to sense her agitation. She sat down at the table. "Maybe you'd like to ride?"

"Ride?" Elise's eyes grew wide. "Do you mean ride, as in ride horses?"

Rosa laughed and nodded.

"I'd love to ride!" Elise was on her feet in an instant, her face flushed with excitement. "I've never ridden before. But I've read all about it. Hundreds of books." She clasped her hands together. "It sounds so wonderful."

"*Bueno*. Run upstairs and change your clothes. I'll take you over to the stables. I'm sure James will be glad to help you. Next to Tanner, he's the best horseman I know."

Elise was halfway through the door when she whirled around, a deep frown marring her face. "Rosa, I'm afraid I don't have a riding costume."

Rosa dried her hands on her towel. "Don't you fret. I've got a skirt or two of my daughter's we can use." She paused to study Elise's trim figure. "They'll fit just fine after we take a tuck or two."

An hour later, Elise emerged from her room, swishing her newly acquired skirt with delight. She paused at the top of the stairs to twirl gracefully on her toes.

"My, don't you look lovely," Rosa called from the foot of the staircase.

"Oh, Rosa!" Elise exclaimed with a start as she clapped a hand over her heart. "I didn't see you down there." She smoothed the front of her skirt self-consciously. "I hope you won't think I'm silly for dancing around. I suppose it's quite improper, but I couldn't resist." She hesitated a moment before explaining. "The skirt is so light, not at all like the mountains of fabric I'm usually wearing. I feel as though I could fly."

"I don't think it's silly at all," Rosa reassured her. "I'm glad you like it."

"It's lovely. Such a pretty shade of orange. I hope your daughter won't mind my borrowing it." Elise descended the stairs while tying the ribbons of her straw bonnet beneath her chin. She could see Rosa staring at her hat. A bright crimson warmed her cheeks. "Is something wrong? Is it my bonnet? Wrong color? I have an awful time with colors. I like pink and turquoise and orange together, so I hoped it would be acceptable." She nibbled her lip in embarrassed uncertainty.

Rosa dragged her eyes from the pink, flower-strewn confection perched on top of Elise's elaborate coiffure to meet her troubled gaze. "Sure, honey, it'll be just fine. This isn't Boston. The folks up there got rules about everything. Texans are more concerned with what's practical. As long as its got a brim to keep the sun off your face, it'll be great."

In truth she thought the ensemble looked a bit on the bright side, but wild horses wouldn't drag it out of her. Poor child seemed insecure enough. Thanks to Aunt Claudia no doubt. "Come on now, honey. James is awaiting you."

Elise followed her through the house and out the back toward the stables. A tall young man, who she guessed to be in his early twenties, appeared at the doorway.

"Hello, James." Rosa made the introductions. "This is Miss Garver, your new student."

James gave a low whistle of appreciation as his eyes roamed over Elise. "Rosa, you didn't tell me how purty she is."

Elise felt herself flush hotly and she studied the ground in embarrassment.

"James has always been one to speak his mind, Elise. Doesn't have a clue as to what's proper with the ladies. You'll have to forgive him." Rosa turned to James. "Now you take good care of her, you hear?"

James gave a broad grin. "It'll be my pleasure." He slid an arm around Elise and guided her toward the stalls. "Ever ridden before?"

She shook her head.

"Then what we need is a real gentle mount." He stroked his chin thoughtfully as he considered the horses, finally coming to a stop in front of a chestnut mare. "I think Miss Sadie will do nicely."

Elise reached up cautiously to stroke the velvety nose of the horse. "She's beautiful."

"You and her's a fine match, Miss Garver. Two beautiful women with hair the color of chestnuts."

Elise smiled at the unusual compliment. She'd never been compared to a horse before. James glowed at her reaction, obviously proud of his prowess with women.

She stood back to watch in fascination as James saddled Miss Sadie and led her from the stall. "Are you ready?" he asked finally.

Elise's eyes opened wide. "Already?" she gulped.

James gave a hearty laugh. "Don't you worry. She's as gentle as a baby." He moved closer to Elise to confide, "And I'm not going to let anything happen to you."

Elise nodded solemnly.

"Ordinarily, folks use a stool to get their foot up in the stirrup, but," he smiled broadly, "in your case, I think it best if I lift you up."

Elise backed up a step. "Oh, I'm not sure that would be at all seemly."

Before she could protest further, James grasped her around the waist and swung her up high into the saddle.

Elise gasped. Sitting atop the horse was unlike anything she'd ever done, and no amount of reading could convey the awesome feeling of towering in the air on the back of a magnificent beast.

"Now relax," James coached. "Hold the horn there in front of you and get your balance." He steadied her until she felt stable. "You okay?"

Elise nodded, her lower lip tucked between her teeth.

"Good. I'm gonna take the reins and lead you around the corral a time or two. When you're ready, I'll give you the reins and you can ride alone."

Elise took a deep breath and nodded again.

The first circle around the corral, Elise clung to the horse for dear life, her knuckles white on the horn. Gradually, she began to relax as her body adjusted to the rhythm of the horse's gait. After a second pass, she mustered enough confidence to signal James she was ready to go it alone.

"Here are the reins. Hold them like this." James placed the leather straps into her hands, lingering a bit longer than necessary. "That's good, now relax your grip. You don't want to hold them quite so tight."

Elise complied, her body tense with concentration.

"Okay, take her around once. And Miss Garver?"

Elise looked up.

"It's okay to smile."

Elise grinned self-consciously. "Thank you, James. I'll try to remember that."

At his command, Miss Sadie obediently began to walk with her pupil around the corral. It was wonderful. Elise reveled in the freedom of sitting up so high, and the knowledge that she was in control. Riding into the cool spring breezes, she'd never felt so alive. With each pass, her confidence grew stronger. Perhaps it would be easier for her father to love her if she could ride well.

She was disappointed to see James finally climb down off the fence where he'd been sitting and move into the ring to join her. She didn't know how long she'd been riding, but she was certain she could have ridden the same path for hours.

"Miss Garver, I think you've had enough for today." He didn't miss the sad little sigh that escaped or the disappointment in her eyes. "I can see that you're having a fine time. Why, I can tell that you have the makings for a real fine horsewoman, but another minute in the saddle and you'll regret it tomorrow."

James took the reins and led them back to the stables. "We'll handle the gettin' off same as the gettin' on."

Elise obediently turned to face him, allowing him to gently lift her from the saddle and place her on her feet. To her astonishment, her legs felt like jelly beneath her and she began to collapse. James came to her rescue by scooping her up against himself.

"That looks like enough lessons for today, James," Tanner thundered from behind them. "I'm sure you have plenty of work to do."

James grinned unabashedly into the scowling face of his boss. "Yessir, you're right. Plenty of work, but nothing that smells this sweet."

Elise disengaged herself from James's supporting arms and struggled to stand alone. She smiled brightly as she tried to adjust her bonnet that now listed heavily to the left.

"Good morning, Tanner." She pushed a stray lock of hair from her eyes. "I hope you won't take Mr. uh, James to task for the time spent on my instruction. I requested it, you see." Her trembling hands overadjusted the bonnet, which now hung precariously over her right ear. "I was in need of a tutor. Up until now, my only experience with horses has been in books and while I have done extensive reading on the subject, I must say that reading about it simply doesn't compare. Do you know—"

"Miss Garver," Tanner growled, "I know that we're running a ranch here, not a baby-sitting service for Boston socialites. So why don't you get yourself up to the house and out of my way."

Elise's eyes flew open in astonishment at the animosity she heard in his voice. For a moment she was speechless. "Thank you, Tanner," her voice was politely cool. "I'll do just that."

She remained only a moment more, to bestow a warm

smile on the man standing beside him. "James, I thank you so much for the lovely morning." With those words, Elise turned and staggered to the house with as much dignity as her wobbly legs would allow.

four

Elise's heart fluttered wildly as she knocked on her father's door late that afternoon. Here was her chance to put her plan in action. She wasn't certain how, but one way or another, she was going to earn his love.

"Good afternoon, sir."

"Good afternoon, Elise." Seth smiled broadly. "Come in and sit down, won't you?"

She moved into the room and took the chair he indicated by the bed. "How are you feeling today?"

"Just fine, thank you. And you? Did you rest well last night?"

"Yes, thank you. My room is very comfortable."

"That's fine."

Father and daughter sat regarding one another, each waiting for the other to speak. Silence stretched between them.

It was Seth that finally spoke. "Rosa tells me you went riding today."

Elise's eyes lit up with the memory. "Oh yes, it was wonderful. I rode Miss Sadie, the chestnut mare. James said she was very gentle." Her voice grew more animated as she continued, "I've read about riding in books, but the written word simply doesn't do justice to actually riding a horse. It gives such a feeling of power. Of course, I didn't go very far, just around the corral, but it was so exciting. Back in Boston—" Elise stopped abruptly. She was rambling again.

Aunt Claudia had warned her time and again that her rambling was annoying and unbecoming to a lady. Not at all proper. Now here she was with her father, trying to win his affection, and instead she was repelling him with her bad manners. Elise stared dejectedly at her hands folded primly in her lap, her lower lip trapped between her teeth.

Seth was puzzled by the sudden change in his daughter. She seemed so happy and then, with the mention of Boston, she became quiet. A fleeting thought saddened him. She must be homesick already. Ready to get back to her life in Boston, her life without him. His smile dissolved into a worried frown.

Elise looked up into the stern face of her father, thinking it was disapproval she saw mirrored there. Her heart sank. Why couldn't she be quiet, like a proper young lady? Hadn't she learned one thing from Mrs. Rhoades's handbook?

Tanner stuck his head inside the door. "Seth, have you got a minute?"

"Sure. Find out anything about the fences?"

"The ones by the south spring were completely destroyed."

"Any clue as to who did it?"

Tanner strode into the room, shaking his head. "None. Must be pretty organized, whoever they are, cuz the rustling problem is countywide. Word is, the Texas Rangers have been called in. Figure they'll have it under control in no time. Meanwhile, I've sent a couple of the boys out to repair—" He stopped as he seemed to notice Elise for the first time. His dark eyes held hers.

Elise recognized the hostile glare from earlier. She rose quickly to her feet, hoping to avoid another confrontation with Tanner, this one in front of her father. She did not need another strike against her. "Will you two excuse me? I need to help Rosa with dinner."

"That's fine, Elise," her father said, nodding to her as she paused in the doorway. "I enjoyed our visit."

ta

"So, Tanner my boy," Seth asked as soon as the door closed behind her, "What do you think of my little girl? She's a real beauty, isn't she?"

"Yes sir, she is."

Seth's brow raised slightly at the begrudging tone of Tanner's voice. Something wasn't quite right here. He pressed on, hoping to get an answer. "She's been riding today. James had her on Miss Sadie. Wished I coulda been there."

Actually, Seth had watched the whole thing from the window of his room, after Rosa had alerted him to the fact that Elise was to ride. His heart had swelled with pride as he watched his precious daughter circle the ring on the back of Miss Sadie. She was nervous, he could see that in her posture, but he could also see a natural grace as she handled the horse. She'd be a fine rider someday.

From his vantage point, he had also seen Tanner watching Elise's progress from the shadows of the stable where he thought he was undetected. "Sure was nice of James to work with her. I figured you musta been busy, otherwise you'd have been the one teaching her. Not a finer horseman than you anywhere."

Tanner refused to meet Seth's gaze as he mumbled

something unintelligible, confirming in Seth's mind the fact that something wasn't quite right between Tanner and his daughter. It was also obvious Tanner wasn't ready to talk about it yet. Seth elected to hold his peace for the time being.

≈

Elise wandered downstairs thoroughly disheartened. Rosa met her at the door of the kitchen.

"Why the long face, honey? I thought you were visiting with your father?"

"He and Tanner had business to discuss, so I left. I thought maybe there was something I could do for you."

Rosa gave her a warm smile. "You can keep me company over a cup of tea while I peel these potatoes for dinner."

Elise sat down at the table, resting her chin on her hands. "May I ask you a question? It's about Tanner."

"Sure, honey." Rosa put two cups on the table then sat down to join her. "What do you want to know?"

"What exactly does he do for my father?"

Rosa chuckled. "Better question would be what doesn't he do. Officially, Tanner's our foreman, but actually, he's much more than that. He's Seth's right-hand man."

"My father seems to like him very much," Elise said, absently tracing the rim of the cup with her finger.

"Tanner's been like a son to Seth, ever since we found him."

Elise quirked a delicate brow. "Found him?"

"That's right," Rosa nodded. "Indians had attacked his family's wagon. Everything was burning when Seth arrived. Seth was able to save Tanner. I'm afraid the rest of the family was lost."

"Oh, Rosa, how awful. He has no one." Elise felt a familiar pang, knowing the pain of being alone.

"That's right, honey, although he and Seth hit it off together real quick. The two of them's inseparable. Seth raised him, and together they built this place."

Elise brushed aside a momentary stab of jealousy. Tanner had found a place where he belonged and someone to care for him. It hurt to know he held the place in her father's heart that she had wanted for herself. Was there room for both? She wondered if she would ever know the peace of belonging and the love and approval of a family.

A dreadful thought occurred to Elise. If she wanted to earn her father's love, it was likely she'd have to gain friendship with Tanner, his right-hand man. She smiled to herself at the incongruity of them being friends. Perhaps a more realistic goal would be securing his tolerance.

The plan was becoming more complex by the hour. And yet it was so simple. Elise would not go back to Boston without knowing her father loved her.

Elise stood up. "Rosa, is there something I can help you with before dinner?"

"No, honey." Rosa smiled up at her. "It's all done."

"Well then, if it's all right with you, I think I'll go on upstairs. I've got lots to do before dinner." Lots of scheming, she added silently.

≈

Elise arrived at dinner, ready to implement her recently amended plan of action to earn Tanner's approval as well as her father's love. She stared in dismay at the table set for two.

Rosa bustled into the room behind her. "There you are.

Dinner's all ready. We may as well get started." She took her place at the table and signaled Elise to join her.

"But my father. . . ?"

"Must take his meals in his room," Rosa finished for her. Elise's face fell. "Oh, I didn't know. Is he that weak?"

Only in his head, Rosa thought. Aloud she said, "The way I figure it, him having to eat in his room might be the strongest medicine for what ails him."

Elise turned an earnest gaze upon her. "Rosa, exactly what is it that ails him?"

Rosa bit her tongue to keep the word "foolishness" from escaping. Instead she merely shook her head. "You'll have to ask him about that."

Elise was thoroughly confused and more than a bit curious. The letter she had received from the doctor had been vague, no specific diagnosis given for her father and now Rosa refused to elaborate. She hoped they weren't merely sheltering her from the truth to protect her.

"Tanner won't be joining us, either?"

"No. He said he's got work to do." Rosa clucked softly as she shook her head. "It's not like him to miss a meal. Must be real worried about the rustling." She noticed the concerned look on Elise's face and decided to change the subject.

"Listen to me chatter while the food's getting cold. I'll ask the blessing and then we can eat." Rosa took Elise's hand in hers and began to pray, "Heavenly Father, I thank You for the food You have provided for us out of Your abundance. Bless it to the nourishment of our bodies. And Father," Rosa continued, "take care of the troubles we're having with the rustlers and our fences so that Seth and

Tanner can quit worrying about them. Finally, Father, I thank You for Elise. Thank You for bringing her here to us. I ask You to guide and direct us in all that we do and say so that You will be glorified. In Jesus' name, Amen."

Rosa looked up to find Elise staring at her in wide-eyed amazement. "Is something wrong?"

Elise shook her head. "No, nothing's wrong. It's just that I've never heard anyone pray like that before."

"Like what?"

"Well," Elise hesitated, searching for the right words, "so conversationally for one thing, like you were actually talking to God."

Rosa giggled. "I was actually talking to God."

Elise blushed. "Well, yes, that's true I guess. Do you always talk to Him about the things going on in your life, like rustlers and fences?"

"Certainly." Rosa studied the awed expression on her companion's face. "Don't you?"

"No," Elise answered matter of factly. "I don't pray at all. Except at church, of course. We have prayer books to read out of on Sunday."

Rosa was clearly shocked. "You don't pray?" she managed to squeak out.

"Not anymore." Elise shook her head. "I used to pray a lot, but God never seemed to answer my prayers." *At least the ones about my father,* she thought. "When I asked Aunt Claudia about it, she said it was because God isn't interested in the minor details of our lives. He has more important things to concern Himself with, like saving sinners and judgment. You know, really big things. She said that's why He gave us minds, to take care of the everyday things."

Rosa was speechless. She had always gone to God about everything. She couldn't imagine being deprived of the peace of mind she had knowing her Heavenly Father was deeply concerned with every area of her life.

With a new resolve in her heart, Rosa passed the heaping plate of fried chicken. Along with the love and affection she was going to shower on Elise, she'd have the privilege of introducing her to the loving care of her Heavenly Father.

❧

Becky scratched her tin plate and gave a plaintive whine.

Tanner looked up from his place at the table and frowned. "Quit your complainin'. That's all you're getting tonight. Fact is, you're looking a little hefty, anyway. A little less food won't hurt you a bit."

She ambled over to the door and barked.

"Forget it. I'm not eating over at the house and neither are you. No way. Not with that Garver woman."

Becky cocked her head slightly, her liquid brown eyes locked on Tanner's face.

"Don't give me that look. I know what you're thinking. That I'm scared of softening. Well, don't give it a second thought. She's trouble and I won't rest until she's gone." Tanner rubbed his lightly stubbled chin. "I owe it to Seth, Becky. Fact is, I scared her off good today—"

A knock at the front door interrupted his discourse. Becky was on her hind legs instantly, yapping excitedly to greet the new arrival.

"Now what?" Tanner muttered ill-naturedly as he swung the door open. He stopped and stared, unable to believe his eyes.

"Good evening, Tanner." Elise smiled tremulously. "I hope I'm not interrupting anything. We had lots of food left over from dinner and I thought, well, we thought you might be hungry. Rosa said fried chicken was your favorite."

Becky gave a soft bark. Elise smiled. "And yours, too, Becky." She looked back to Tanner who continued to stare at her without speaking. He didn't look nearly so fierce without his black hat, she thought with relief. Perhaps he wasn't quite so angry with her anymore.

When she had mentioned fixing a plate up for him to Rosa, she hadn't intended to be the one to deliver it.

"That's a wonderful idea, Elise," Rosa had said. "I'll fix up a couple of plates, and you can carry them over real quick while I clean up the dishes."

Elise couldn't very well deny her. How could she explain the problem between her and Tanner when she didn't understand it herself. She tried to refuse on the grounds that it was improper for a lady to visit a man at his home without a suitable chaperone, but her protests fell on deaf ears. Rosa would not be swayed. Mrs. Rhoades and her rules of propriety didn't seem to hold the same importance here in Texas as they did in Boston.

Fortunately, her fear of facing him appeared unfounded. Though he continued to stare at her with a look of disbelief, he had not berated her or sent her away. Her hopes raised slightly. Maybe one day they'd be friends, after all.

"If it's all right, I'll just leave the plates here and let you get back to work."

Tanner found his voice. "Work? Oh, yeah, work." He ran a hand through his hair. "Had lots to do tonight. Didn't feel like I could get away."

Elise smiled and nodded. "I understand completely." She waited for him to step aside so she could pass. He seemed rooted to the floor. "May I come in?"

"In? Sure, that's fine." Tanner frantically scanned the room, trying to see it through the eyes of a stranger. His eyes fell upon the pair of boots he had deposited in the middle of the floor. He walked over to them and bent casually to retrieve them, quickly stashing them out of sight behind the sofa.

"You have a lovely home," Elise said as she followed him inside.

"Thanks. Seth built it for your mother."

"My mother? Lived here?" Elise's voice was reverent. She laid the plates on the table and turned to survey the room more carefully.

It was more of a cottage than a house, with one large, general purpose room, one half serving as a kitchen and the other as a living room. She guessed that the door in the back led to the sleeping area. The furnishings were simple, as befitting a man, but comfortable.

"It's just lovely." Elise heard her voice break slightly. It was so special to be in the very home where her mother had once lived. She wanted to sit down and close her eyes, to let her imagination fill the house with the family she never knew.

Becky barked, startling Elise back to the present. "Oh, I really must be going. I hadn't intended to detain you." She pulled the towels off the plates. "Come, sit down and eat before it gets cold." Elise stepped toward the door. "I can let myself out. Enjoy your dinner. Good night."

Tanner said nothing as she pulled the door closed behind her. He continued to stare at the doorway for a long time until Becky's insistent scratching at his leg caught his attention.

"You can just wipe that silly grin off your face, fool dog. Nothin's changed. I couldn't hardly throw her out after she was so nice to bring us dinner." He placed Becky's plate on the floor, shaking his head in mild frustration. "I gotta admit, it would be a whole lot easier if she was mean and ugly."

five

Elise sat on the edge of her bed in complete misery. Yesterday's ride had taken it's toll just as James had predicted. Her legs and backside were so stiff and sore, she couldn't decide what hurt worse, sitting or standing.

She managed to dress herself, but she was not altogether certain that she could navigate the flight of stairs. She knew she'd have to come down eventually; Rosa would worry if she didn't make it to breakfast and Elise was mortified at the idea of being discovered. Her soreness was proof positive that she was nothing more than a Boston socialite.

Summoning all her strength, she maneuvered slowly and painfully down the stairs to the kitchen where Becky's familiar black form reclined by the door, indicating that her master was present.

"Good morning," she called with forced cheerfulness. "Sorry I'm late."

"Come sit down, honey," Rosa hopped up and headed to the stove. "I've got your breakfast all ready."

Elise hoped they wouldn't notice her stiff-legged gait as she hobbled to the table. "Smells delicious, Rosa." She pasted a smile on her face as she gingerly lowered herself to the chair, but she couldn't help wincing as the hard wood connected with her wounded flesh.

She fought back the hot tears that stung in her eyes,

knowing instinctively that Tanner's dark gaze was following her every movement. She couldn't let him see that she was hurting. It would simply confirm all the bad things he thought of her.

Rosa placed a full plate in front of her, completely unaware of her discomfort. "Bet you're anxious to get out there riding again this morning. James was bragging to me what a fine rider you are. Says you show a lot of promise."

Elise nibbled her lower lip. "Well, uh. . . ."

"No, she won't be riding today," Tanner pronounced. Elise jerked her head up with a start and stared into his face. Their eyes locked as he continued, "I need James to help me with the fences."

Elise rewarded him with a dazzling smile. Without knowing it, he had just saved her hide, literally.

Rosa however, didn't share Elise's enthusiasm. "Now Tanner, surely you could spare him for an hour or so." Her dark eyes were pleading. "James says she's a natural."

"I'm sorry, Rosa." Tanner got to his feet, hat in hand. "I can't spare him today. Too much work to do."

"I guess I can find someone else to work with her."

Tanner shook his head. "Seth would skin me if I let her ride without James or myself. Miss Garver doesn't ride today."

"Well," Rosa answered a bit huffily, "if you insist."

Rosa missed the wink Tanner directed at Elise before he disappeared through the doorway. "Maybe tomorrow," he called over his shoulder. "If she's up to it."

Elise blushed furiously, partially because it was painfully obvious that Tanner had discovered her secret. But a portion of the warmth she felt diffuse through her was directly attributable to the handsome man himself. Had he actually forbidden her to ride in order to protect her? Was it possible he might like her just a little bit ,after all? And why did that thought hold so much appeal?

"He can be so stubborn when he wants to be," Rosa complained. "I'm sorry about the riding, honey. Maybe you'd like to help me plant my kitchen garden this morning instead?"

Elise was still in a daze. "Sure, Rosa, that sounds just fine."

ta

Several hours later, after having spent the morning in the garden, Elise slowly ascended the stairs. Her back and head now ached along with the rest of her anatomy, her only thought was to make it to her comfortable bed where she could collapse and die.

She pulled the bedroom door closed behind her and dropped, fully clothed, onto the bed. In a matter of minutes, she drifted off into an exhausted slumber.

ta

"Good afternoon, Father," said Elise.

"Oh, Elise, come in." Seth closed the ledger he was reading. "I didn't hear you."

Elise paused in the doorway. "Am I interrupting something?" Perhaps I should come back later."

"No, no indeed. Just looking over the books." Seth smiled up at his daughter. "Sit down."

Elise eyed the chair warily. "I think I'd prefer to stand if you don't mind."

Seth shrugged. "Fine with me. So tell me, did you have a nice day?"

"Yes, sir. Rosa and I put in her kitchen garden."

"Good, good. Nice weather for planting, not too warm."

"Yes, sir, very nice. Quite comfortable, actually."

Seth nodded and smiled. Elise nodded and smiled. Then silence.

The clock, ticking in the background, reminded her of how quickly her time with her father was fleeing. If she didn't implement her plan soon, all would be lost. How could she make him love her if they didn't speak. The proper thing to do would be to wait until he spoke, to let him initiate the conversation. But being proper was getting her nowhere. Perhaps she should risk taking a chance.

"So, you were looking over the books," she began hesitantly. "Is there a lot of bookkeeping involved with ranching?"

She was delighted to see he did not seem annoyed by the question. On the contrary, he appeared to be pleased.

"Depends on the rancher, I suppose. I like to keep up with the expenses, of course, and I keep close tabs on how many head of cattle I've got."

Elise's heart soared. She could tell by the sparkle in his eyes that this subject was something in which he was interested. Since horses had become a painful subject, perhaps the operations of the ranch could be their common ground. "How many head of cattle do you have?"

A brisk knock on the door interrupted his answer.

Tanner strolled across the floor to Seth's side. "I got those numbers you were looking for. Cattle prices look better than ever."

Elise was crestfallen. She and her father were actually talking, not just exchanging meaningless pleasantries. She didn't want to leave. Perhaps she could stay and listen to the men talk business.

She nibbled her lower lip while studying the two men in conversation. Suppose in the course of the discussion, Tanner decided to share with her father the fact that she was practically incapacitated by her ride yesterday. She couldn't bear it. She didn't want her father to think she was just a Boston socialite. She wanted him to be proud of her. She wanted him to love her.

Maybe if she disappeared, her name wouldn't come up. "If you will excuse me." Elise walked stiffly to the door. "I need to get ready for dinner."

"Fine, Elise, thank you for coming."

Both men watched as she closed the door behind her.

੨੦

"Evenin', Rosa." Tanner strode into the kitchen with Becky following close on his heels. He wrapped his arms around Rosa, squeezing her in a bone-crushing embrace. "Dinner smells delicious. We're starved."

Rosa beamed up into his handsome face. "Go on and sit down. I'll get it on the table right away."

He sat down at the empty table and asked casually, "Where's our little city kid tonight?"

Rosa laid a full plate in front of him. "She's not coming down. Says she's not hungry." She sat down with a worried sigh. "The child hasn't been herself today."

"What do you mean?" Tanner's dark eyes met hers, his brows suddenly furrowed with concern.

Rosa shrugged. "I don't know exactly. She just seemed real sluggish. Almost like it pained her to move."

Tanner thought of Elise's behavior at breakfast. He

recognized clearly the signs that she had spent a bit too much time in the saddle. The thought was actually amusing to him at the time. *Fact is,* he figured, *she deserved it. She doesn't belong here, anyway.*

Tonight, however, he found himself strangely disappointed that she wouldn't be joining them for dinner. For a city kid, she had a lot of gumption. She must be in more pain than he had realized.

Seeing that Elise hadn't explained the source of her discomfort to Rosa, Tanner opted not to mention it, either. "Rosa, I wouldn't worry if I were you. It just takes city folks a few days to settle in. That's all."

"Do you think so?" Rosa's voice was hopeful. "I wish I could help her."

"I'll bet a hot bath would fix her up just fine."

"A hot bath?"

Tanner grinned broadly. "Trust me on this one."

"If you really think so." She studied Tanner's face to be certain he was serious. Satisfied that he was, she got up from the table. "I'll start heating the water up right away."

೭

After dinner, Tanner left the house and Rosa continued to prepare Elise's bath. "Elise, honey," Rosa called softly into Elise's darkened bedroom, "I've got a nice hot bath ready for you downstairs."

Elise pushed herself up into a sitting position on the bed to look at Rosa. "A hot bath?" If it wouldn't have been so painful, she'd have jumped for joy. "That sounds wonderful. I'll be right down."

She gathered her soap and powder and a dressing gown from the wardrobe, and descended the stairs as quickly as

she could on her stiff legs. Rosa led her to a small room off
the kitchen with a huge tub in the center. Elise could see
steam rising from the water.

In no time at all, Elise undressed, pinned her long hair up
on top of her head, and lowered herself slowly into the tub
with a delighted sigh. Submerged in the steamy liquid, she
could feel her stiffness melting away.

For a long time, she was absolutely still, savoring the delicious warmth. Finally, as the water began to cool, she
reached for the bar of soap. She hummed a happy tune while
working it into a frothy lather, its flowery fragrance filling
the air.

Tanner swung open the back door and stepped into the
house. He had forgotten his hat at dinner and had come to
retrieve it. A familiar fragrance wafting down the hall
stopped him in his tracks—flowers, a whole field of flowers.
He breathed deeply of the heady aroma.

Even though the door was closed, he could hear Elise
humming cheerfully as she splashed around in the next
room. He paused for a minute or two, enchanted by the sound
of her voice. Finally, he forced himself to move down the
hall to the dining room, his heart inexplicably lighter with
the knowledge that the little socialite felt better.

After Elise had dried herself off and dressed in her robe,
she padded into the kitchen where Rosa was seated at the
table. "Rosa, I can't thank you enough for fixing the bath
for me. It was exactly what I needed."

Rosa smiled up at her. "I'm so glad, *querida*. But I'm
afraid the thanks should go to Tanner. The bath was his
idea."

"Tanner?" Elise squeaked, wrapping her dressing gown

around herself more tightly. "It was Tanner's idea?"

Rosa nodded, oblivious to Elise's distress. "He seemed to think it would be a real tonic for you. And I can see that he was right." She pointed to the stove. "Are you hungry? Can I fix you a piece of pie?"

"No, I think not." Elise shook her head. "I'm awfully sleepy. I'll just go on up to bed."

"Fine, honey. Oh, by the way, do you remember our conversation last night, about talking to God about all the little details in our lives?"

Elise nodded.

"I was reading in my Bible tonight, and I found a couple of verses that helped me to see that God cares about all the details in our lives." She picked up the worn book resting on the table in front of her. "I wrote them on a piece of paper. Maybe if you get a chance, you can look them up."

"Thank you." With a smile, Elise accepted the Bible from her. "That was very kind of you."

Rosa got to her feet and pressed a kiss onto Elise's cheek. "Sleep well, *querida*." Rosa breathed a silent prayer as she watched the young woman leave. *Heavenly Father, I've shown her the truth. It's up to You to help her believe it.*

Elise lay back against the cool sheets, up in her bed, wondering if she should be elated or mortified. That a man should suggest she take a bath was truly beyond the bounds of propriety. Poor Aunt Claudia would be apoplectic if she knew.

On the other hand, the bath had truly worked miracles on her abused flesh. How thoughtful of him to be concerned. Elise pulled the covers up under her chin. Was it possible? Was Tanner concerned about her?

Not likely, she told herself. Yesterday's tongue lashing was still fresh on her mind. He made it clear that he wanted her as faraway from him as possible.

However, she argued, hadn't he prevented her from riding this morning? And wasn't he the one who suggested a bath for her tonight? She was no expert, but that sounded like concern to her.

Elise drifted off to sleep, smiling at the thought.

six

Elise's long dark lashes flickered against her cheeks. The sun peeked through the lace curtains, beckoning her to awaken to a new day. Her first thought was about her stiffness. Would she spend another day in agony?

Ever so carefully, she gave a tiny stretch, testing her arms. To her relief, they felt fine. Next, she flexed her legs. Again, no pain. She pulled back the covers and sat up. Other than an awareness of her backside, she felt completely normal.

She stood up with the intention of getting dressed when the Bible that Rosa had given her last night caught her eye. She picked it up off the bedstand and flipped to one of the passages that Rosa had marked.

The first one was Matthew 10:29-30, and Jesus was speaking. " 'Are not two aparrows sold for a farthing? and one of them shall not fall on the ground without your Father. but the very hairs of your head are all numbered.' "

Elise read the passage again. She'd been attending church every Sunday of her life and yet she had never heard this Scripture. God knew the number of hairs on her head? She absently twirled a silky lock on her finger. That sure sounded like He was interested in little details about her. And the part about the sparrows. She had no idea God kept up with birds, too.

For a moment, Elise disputed the truth of what she had read. After all, if it was true, wouldn't she have heard it before now? Why hadn't their minister told them? Her eyes were drawn back to the Scripture. It was Jesus speaking: God's son. She knew He did not lie. And Who better than He to tell just exactly what God was interested in.

The second passage Rosa had written down was found in Philippians. Elise fumbled through the pages until she found the fourth chapter. "Be careful for nothing; but in every thing by prayer and supplication with thanksgiving let your requests be made known unto God." Rosa had scribbled a note in the margin: Paul tells us if it is important enough for you to care about, it is important enough to share with God. He wants to bear all our burdens, nothing is too small, so turn your cares into prayers.

Elise sat down on the edge of the bed. Paul, too, seemed to be convinced that God was interested in the day-to-day details of His children's lives. Paul didn't say that God takes care of salvation and judgment and you take care of the rest. It sounded to her as though God wanted to hear about it all.

It was late, and Elise's stomach rumbled, urging her to get downstairs for breakfast, but she delayed a moment longer to read a final verse in 1 Peter 5:7. "Casting all your care upon him, for he careth for you." Here it was again. Another directive to place all of one's burdens on God. The verse even explained why—because God cares. She sighed as she closed the book, replacing it on the table. What a thought. God cares.

Rosa was clearing away the dishes when Elise finally arrived in the kitchen.

"There you are! I was afraid you weren't feeling well this morning."

Elise smiled. "I feel fine. I got interested reading in your Bible and lost track of the time." She eyed the stove hopefully. "Any more coffee?"

"Sure is. And biscuits, too. They're warming in the oven."

Elise placed two fluffy biscuits on a plate and sat at the table. Rosa joined her with a cup of coffee for each of them.

"So what did you think? I mean about the Bible verses?"

"It's all right there, just as you said." Elise spread a liberal dollop of butter on one of her biscuits. "Each one of them seemed to point clearly to the fact that God is indeed concerned with every area of our lives."

She bit into the biscuit and chewed thoughtfully. "But you know, Rosa, I used to pray. I prayed faithfully, every single day about something very important thing to me, and yet He never answered my prayer."

Rosa was at a loss for words as she studied the intense, emerald gaze directed at her. James's sudden appearance in the kitchen made it impossible for her to continue.

"Good morning," he began, beaming at Elise. "Is my student ready for another day in the saddle?"

"James," Rosa intervened, "I haven't had a chance to tell her you called for her already this morning. She just now got downstairs. Maybe you can come back later."

Elise popped the last of the biscuit into her mouth. "Oh, no, don't go. I'm ready now. I just need to get my hat." She hopped up from the table. "Thanks for breakfast, Rosa." She was halfway down the hall when she called out, "I'll only be just a minute, James."

Minutes later the two of them crossed the yard to the stables, Elise skipping alongside him in her excitement. "I'm looking forward to my ride this morning. Will it be

Miss Sadie again? We worked so well together, I thought. I don't think I'll be quite so nervous."

James laughed at her enthusiastic chatter. "I figured you'd be wantin' Miss Sadie. I got her all saddled and ready for ya." He stopped for a moment, licking his lips nervously. "May I say, Miss Garver, you're looking mighty colorful this morning."

Elise smiled self-consciously. "Thank you. I hoped I wouldn't look silly. I have the most difficult time knowing which colors to wear together. My Aunt Claudia always says I'm as thick as a post when it comes to colors."

"Tain't true, Miss Garver. Why, God Himself puts all them colors together in the rainbow."

Elise couldn't resist a smile. "I never thought about it that way before. I guess you're right."

Encouraged by his success, James pressed on. "And that's a right fine bonnet yer wearin'. Why I bet every bee in the county will be plum delighted over all them flowers. It's like a regular garden, just sittin' on your head."

She smiled again. James, immeasurably pleased with himself, puffed out his chest and strutted into the darkened stable with Elise following close behind. She stepped aside to allow him to lead Miss Sadie from the stall.

"Here she is. Lemme give you a lift up and we'll get started." He stepped toward Elise with his arms extended.

"Thank you, James." Tanner's deep voice rang out from the entrance. "I'll be taking care of Miss Garver's instruction today." He and Becky joined them in front of the stall.

James's face fell at the interruption. "Aw, Tanner, why did ya have to come in now? This here's the best part."

Elise was unable to see the exchange between the two men, but she suspected Tanner of applying his chillingly dark glare to James. Whatever it was, James decided not to protest further. "Okay, boss, I've got lots to do, anyway." He shrugged his shoulders. "See you later, Miss Garver."

"Tanner, I'm. . .surprised. . . ," Elise stammered once they were alone. "I mean, I didn't expect. . . ."

"I had some extra time today." Tanner refused to meet her gaze as he fumbled for an explanation. "Besides, James has plenty to do."

Honestly, he didn't have a clue as to why he volunteered to help her. He certainly had not planned to. He had more than enough to do without wasting time on a frivolous socialite. But here he was.

"I brought something I thought might help," he said quietly, producing a small suede object from behind his back.

"How nice," she answered politely as she studied it with interest. "What is it?"

"A pillow. For your uh, uh, well, you know." Tanner dropped his glance to the floor of the stable. "For sitting on."

Elise felt the crimson stain scorch her skin as it swept across her body. This new infraction was positively unthinkable. No one in polite society ever discussed, even alluded to this sort of thing. And yet. . . , She looked over to Tanner, the ferocious, towering cowboy whose dark gaze struck fear in her heart.

He didn't look too fearsome right now. He was staring at his boots in what looked to Elise to be mortification. Something deep within Elise began to stir and she began to laugh. It started small with a breathless giggle, then blossomed into a full-blown laugh that brought tears to her eyes.

Tanner regretted his words the minute they escaped from his lips. He knew it wasn't the sort of thing one mentioned in front of a lady. What was he thinking, anyway, bringing a pillow for Elise. He had never felt like such an idiot in his life. He was formulating an apology when he heard the lilting sound of her laughter.

He looked up to stare at her in complete disbelief. She was actually laughing. . .hard. Tears glistened in her eyes and one or two were rolling down her silken cheeks.

Tanner was so relieved at her totally unexpected response that he smiled. Her mirth proved infectious and he found himself joining in the laughter. Becky added to the merriment of the twosome with shrill barks of delight.

"What's goin' on in here?" James called from the doorway of the stables. "You two sound like a pack of coyotes. What's so funny, anyway?"

Both Elise and Tanner sobered instantly with his appearance. Elise's hand flew over her mouth in alarm at their discovery. She would rather die than reveal the source of their amusement.

Tanner seemed to sense her concern. "It's nothin'," he called back.

"Didn't sound like nothin' to me," James grumbled as he went back to work.

Elise exhaled loudly, releasing the breath she'd been holding.

Tanner smiled down at her, his dark eyes still glittering with mirth. "Perhaps we should get on with the lessons then?"

Elise nodded.

He placed his hands at her waist and lifted her as though she were weightless, positioning her gently on the pillow-topped saddle. Elise drew a sharp breath. Partially with the pleasure of being atop the horse and partially with the pleasure of being held in Tanner's strong arms.

Tanner heard her draw the breath and mistook it for pain. "Are you all right?" His eyes reflected genuine concern as they searched hers for the answer.

Elise was mesmerized, held captive by their inky depths. For a long moment she could neither think nor speak. Finally, with a small shake of her head, she broke from the spell. "I. . .I'm fine." Her voice sounded shaky to her own ears.

Tanner, too, seemed strangely disturbed. "Good. That's good," he said absently. "Now, what were we talking about?" He pushed his hat back farther on his head. "Oh yeah. Lessons. I think for today, you should stay in the corral and work on form and control. Tomorrow you can start taking Sadie out on the ranch."

"Sounds fine to me."

Tanner took the reins and guided Miss Sadie into the corral. "You need to use your legs when you ride," he instructed. "It's their job to keep you in the saddle, instead of bouncing up and down. I'm afraid you are familiar with the results of bouncing."

Elise nodded sheepishly, her lower lip caught between her teeth.

He folded his arms across his chest as he circled the horse to consider his student. "Your posture looks good. You have good tension on the reins. I think you're ready.

Remember, use your legs." With that final directive, he inclined his head slightly, signaling her to ride.

Elise and Miss Sadie went through the paces with Tanner standing in the center of the ring to offer his suggestions. She was elated at the end of the hour of walking and trotting, starting and stopping, when Tanner pronounced her ready to ride around the ranch.

"That sounds wonderful." She was beaming as she reined in the horse beside him. "It's a beautiful day for it."

Tanner shook his head. "No, I'm afraid you misunderstand. You're finished for the day. An hour in the saddle, even with padding, is more than enough for a city girl. Tomorrow's plenty soon enough."

Elise was too delighted by the way he referred to her as a city girl to offer any protest for the delay. It wasn't the words, but rather the way he said them, as though she were a fragile prize. "Tomorrow sounds just fine."

He reached up for her, and their eyes met and held as she leaned forward, her hands resting lightly on his broad shoulders. Ever so slowly he lowered her to the ground, their eye contact unbroken.

She knew she should remove her hands from him once she felt her feet touch the ground, but she could not. Tanner's hands remained fastened around her waist. For a long silent moment, they stood there, eyes locked, unmoving. His dark gaze drifted to her lips. Elise's heart began to thunder wildly in her chest and her mouth suddenly went dry.

"Hey, boss man! You want me to put Miss Sadie away for ya?"

James's sudden appearance had the effect of an icy

shower. Instantly, the couple separated. Elise dusted the front of her skirt, while Tanner shoved his hands deep into his pockets and kicked at the dirt with his boot.

"That's fine, James." Tanner's deep voice cracked slightly. "We were just finishing up."

James laughed. "Yes, sir. I could see that real plain."

Elise felt the familiar rush of warmth spread across her face. "I need to get on inside." She studied her hands clasped before her, refusing to meet Tanner's eyes as she continued, "Thank you so much for the lessons, Tanner. I've learned a great deal today." With that, she turned heel and practically ran for the house.

"Look, Tanner, I'm real sorry about Miss Garver. I had no idea that you two were, uh, sweethearts. I hope you don't take offense to me riding with her the other day. It was nothing, really."

"No offense taken." Tanner watched as James led Miss Sadie toward the stable. Becky moved over to take her place beside him, rubbing against his leg.

He swept the hat from his head and ran his hands through the dark waves. "Don't bother to ask me what I'm doing, Becky, cuz I don't have any idea."

seven

"Good afternoon, Father." Elise let herself into the room. Her father was in his customary position, propped up against a wall of pillows. "You're looking fit."

"Thank you, Elise. And may I say that you are looking particularly lovely today. Texas must agree with you."

"Thank you, sir." She settled primly into the chair by his bed. "I believe it does."

"Did you enjoy your ride today? Rosa tells me you had another lesson."

Elise stared off into space. "Tanner was wonderful," she said with a dreamy sigh. Her eyes flew open when she realized what she'd said. "What I mean to say is, Tanner is a wonderful instructor." She stared dismally into her lap and tried again. "That is, he seems to be very knowledgeable about horses."

Seth suppressed a chuckle. This morning, he had been at the window, watching with interest as his daughter and Tanner talked together. He hadn't detected the usual animosity. In fact, from where he was sitting, it looked like the opposite. He only wondered if things were truly as they appeared from one story up. Elise's discomfort had given him his answer.

"Yes, he is. Very capable man. I place you in his hands with complete confidence." He wanted to snicker at his little joke, but held his tongue. At that moment, he looked up to see Tanner, standing in the doorway. "Well, speaking of Tanner, here he is. Come on in, son, we were just talking about you."

"Afternoon Seth, Miss Garver." Tanner nodded to both of them as he crossed the room with several long strides. "Rosa told me you wanted to see me."

Seth nodded. "That's true. I want you to look over some of my projected figures for cattle sales. But first, I'd like to thank you for helping Elise with her riding today. She was just telling me what an excellent instructor you are."

Elise had already determined that no matter what the interruption, she would not be driven from her father's room today. In the time she'd spent in Texas, she was no closer to her goal of earning her father's love. She hadn't even had a good conversation with him.

But the sight of Tanner evaporated her resolve. Just looking at him gave her the queerest feeling in her stomach. She actually felt a bit giddy. She had no doubt that if she opened her mouth to speak, something inane would spill out. She couldn't take the chance. She would have to catch her father alone.

"I'll be running along then." She stood up and offered a smile to her father. "I'll be back, same time tomorrow."

"I'm looking forward to it, Elise."

❧

By the time Elise arrived downstairs for dinner, she had time to analyze her strange reaction to Tanner. It was obvious, she decided, that the lightheadedness and butterflies were nothing more than elation over securing his friendship, the first step toward the realization of her dream. It seemed reasonable. After all, hadn't that been part of her plan? To secure Tanner's approval as well as her father's.

She suspected that his dark, ruggedly handsome good looks might be responsible in part for the giddiness; after all, she was only human. But then she reassured herself that it was largely the pleasure of his friendship that left her feeling somewhat addled in his presence.

Fortified with the knowledge that she and Tanner were indeed becoming friends, she faced dinner with complete confidence. The food Rosa prepared was delicious, and the conversation between the three of them was light, making the evening a success.

There was only one awkward moment, when Elise's fingers accidentally met Tanner's as she passed him the platter of beef, and a flash of energy coursed through her. Her surprised reaction had been to withdraw her hand immediately, as though she'd been burned, and the platter would have fallen, had not Tanner caught it. Fortunately for her, no one seemed to notice her blunder.

After everyone had eaten their fill of pie and coffee, Tanner pushed back in his chair. "It's gettin' late." His voice sounded reluctant. "Guess Becky and I better get back to the house, and let you ladies get some rest."

At the signal, both Rosa and Elise got to their feet.

"I surely had a nice time, surrounded by you young people," Rosa said as she scooped several plates off the table and headed for the kitchen. "It was good to have the both of you at dinner for a change." She called over her shoulder, "*Buenas noches*, Tanner. We'll be seeing you in the morning."

"I want to thank you again for my riding lesson today,"

Elise said once they were alone. She lowered her eyes to add, "I enjoyed it very much."

"It was my pleasure." He dropped his hat onto his head and added with a wicked grin, "And if the pillow did the trick, we'll have you riding out on the ranch tomorrow."

Elise couldn't help but return the smile. "Good night, Tanner."

"Good night, Miss Garver. Sleep well."

She watched as he and Becky walked down the hall to the back door. Once they were out of sight, she picked up several dishes from the table and carried them into the kitchen.

"Thank you for dinner, Rosa. It was delicious."

"I'm so glad you liked it, honey." The two women moved back to the dining room together to collect the remainder of the dishes. "You know, Elise," Rosa said as they worked, "I was thinking about what you told me this morning, about not having your prayers answered, and I wanted to ask you a question."

"Certainly."

"Are you a Christian?"

Elise stopped, frozen in her tracks, her green eyes flashing with shocked indignation. "Of course I am," she huffed. "I have attended church every Sunday of my life for as long as I can remember, and," she raised her chin a fraction, "I was elected the recording secretary of the Ladies Missionary Society." Suddenly, she didn't look quite so self-assured. "Is there something about my conduct that would lead you to believe otherwise?

"No indeed, your conduct is just fine," Rosa soothed. "I can see that you are a fine young woman. But some good folks, even those that are members of a church and go every Sunday aren't Christians at all."

Elise was somewhat mollified. She followed Rosa back into the kitchen. "I'm not sure I know what you mean."

"Take yourself for example. You went into the stables today, didn't you?"

"Well, yes."

"Did it make you a horse?"

Elise giggled. "Rosa, that's silly."

"Yes it is, but it makes a point. Just going to church doesn't make you a Christian any more than going to a stable makes you a horse."

Elise looked puzzled. "Then how do you become a Christian?"

"Simple, really," Rosa said as she plunged a plate into the tubful of soapy water. "By making a personal commitment to Jesus."

Elise took the plate that Rosa had washed and rinsed, and dried it with a towel. A worried frown troubled her features. For the first time in the conversation, she wondered if she were, indeed, a Christian.

She couldn't recall ever making a personal commitment, not to Jesus, not to anything. Fact was, Aunt Claudia made most of her commitments for her. Aunt Claudia had chosen the church they attended, the friends that she kept; Aunt Claudia was even the one to choose the position of recording secretary for Elise. Elise merely did as she was told.

"I wonder if you could be more specific," Elise suggested as she took another dripping plate.

"I'll try." Rosa's dark eyes darted around the room, as

she sought inspiration. Her gaze came to rest on the stack of dirty dishes in front of her and she smiled. "You see this plate?" She held up a dinner plate that was streaked with leftover food and gravy. "This is like our lives, all dirty and messy with sin."

Elise giggled at the illustration.

"God wants us to be all pure and clean, so we can be His children. And we want to be His children, because the Bible is full of the many wonderful promises God makes to His children. One of those promises is that He hears their prayers.

"So, we try to clean ourselves up to be worthy of God; like trying to be real good, or attending church regularly, but it doesn't work. We can't make ourselves clean." Rosa took a rag and swished it over the face of the plate, smearing the mess even worse.

"So God sent His only Son, Jesus, to wash away our sins. But our cleanliness came at a very high price. It cost Jesus His life, a sinless life He offered on the cross."

Rosa caught the look of distress on Elise's face. "Jesus was glad to do it, though, because He knew that by taking the punishment we deserved for our sins, we would be cleansed, and we could be God's children." Rosa dipped the plate into the sudsy water and scrubbed it. Then she poured clear water over the plate, rinsing it sparkling clean.

"I've heard all that before, I mean the part about Jesus being crucified for our sins and then being raised from the dead three days later. But I still don't see where the personal commitment part comes in."

"Just knowing the facts isn't enough. You've got to believe them. You have got to believe that Jesus is God's

Son and that He died on the cross for your sins. You have to accept His sacrifice on your behalf and confess Jesus as your Savior."

For a long moment, Elise was silent. She finished drying the plates Rosa handed her, and then stacked them with the others. While she worked, she replayed the conversation over in her mind. She had not known her need for a Savior until now, but once exposed, she felt it acutely. She couldn't wait another minute. In a very small voice, she said, "Rosa, I'd like to make that commitment to Jesus. I want to be one of God's children."

Rosa beamed. "Then let's pray." She must have noticed the crimson blush on Elise's cheeks because she added, "Why don't I pray and you can pray along with me?"

Elise's face mirrored her relief.

Rosa took Elise's hands in hers and bowed her head to pray. "Lord Jesus, I know that I'm a sinner. I thank You for dying on the cross for me, taking my punishment so that I could be forgiven. I ask You to forgive me now. I accept Your sacrifice on my behalf and confess You as my Savior. Thank You for making me a child of God."

A comforting warmth spread through Elise as she whispered the heartfelt prayer. She knew instantly that God had heard. The warmth changed quickly to an unspeakable joy that flooded her from head to toe, dazzling her with its intensity.

Elise was horrified at her own impropriety. Joy? Religion was no place for frivolous emotions. She learned early that church was a place for solemnity and one's spirituality could be accurately gauged by the degree of dourness reflected in one's face. Elise secretly suspected that Aunt Claudia's reputation as a pillar of the church was largely based on her ability to scowl.

She squeezed her eyes closed more tightly, trying to suppress the errant feeling. She'd best carefully school her expression to one of cheerlessness before opening them to meet those of Rosa. She didn't want Rosa to see her grinning like a fool; she might think her prayer had not been sincere.

Finally satisfied that her own expression was one of appropriate gloom, Elise opened her eyes a crack to steal a glance at Rosa. Rosa positively glowed. Her smile was so wide and bright it almost hurt to look at it.

A giggle escaped before Elise could catch it. Another followed, and then another until the two women fell into each others arms, laughing and crying tears of joy.

≥

Tanner lay in bed, his arms folded behind his head. As was customary since the arrival of the Garver woman, he found it difficult to sleep.

"I got it figured out!" he suddenly exclaimed into the darkness. "Becky, old girl, I know what I was doing this afternoon. I was switching strategies!"

At the sound of her name, Becky stopped scratching and looked over toward the bed.

"Sure, that's exactly what I was doing." He rolled over onto his side to face the dog. "What's the best way to get to know the enemy? To spend time with them, right? Well, that's what I was doing. By riding with Miss Garver, I was able to study her at close range, to see what she is really all about."

Seeing he had nothing for her, Becky went back to

scratching at the flea that was annoying her.

"You don't believe me, do you? You think I'm falling for her. Well, don't you worry, Becky. I'm no fool. Those green eyes and the smell of flowers lay a pretty fine trap, but it would take more than that to turn my head. I'm going in with my eyes wide open."

Becky shifted positions in order to reach the flea now lurking on her hind leg.

Tanner was silent for a minute before he spoke again. "I wonder, Becky, while we're on the subject of Miss Garver, did you happen to notice what a fine sense of humor she has? I mean, it takes a big person to be able to laugh at herself.

Becky got to her feet and ambled off into the other room.

"And gumption," he called after her retreating figure. "For a city kid, she's got gumption."

He rolled back onto his back. "Don't worry, though. I've got my eyes wide open."

eight

Elise could scarcely wait to get to breakfast. She raced down the stairs with what she knew to be indecent haste and burst breathlessly into the kitchen. "Good morning, Rosa."

Rosa gathered her into her arms for a hug. "Good morning. And how's the new Christian this morning?"

Elise beamed. "Wonderful, thank you." Her eyes darted around the room. "Where's Tanner?"

"He and a couple of the hands went to check out the cattle. He ought to be back around lunch."

"Oh." Elise was strangely disappointed.

"Something wrong?"

"Oh no, it's just that I thought he was going to teach me to ride today. He said I could go out on the ranch."

Rosa grinned. "That must be why he told me to pack up a picnic. He's figuring on you two getting hungry during the lessons."

"A picnic?" Elise squealed as her heart gave a little jump. "Oh, Rosa!" Her hands flew to her face. "I need to get ready."

Rosa laughed and shook her head as the girl bolted excitedly from the room. "Tanner and Elise? That's something I won't believe till I see it," she declared to the empty room.

The morning dragged on interminably for Elise. She wrote another letter to Aunt Claudia, though she'd already written and mailed one during the course of her short stay. Since little had happened, the letter was quickly written and Elise was again at a loss for something to do.

She thought she might read a bit from Rosa's Bible, but her eyes and mind refused to cooperate.

Even sewing seemed to be beyond Elise. She tried to pick up her much-neglected needlework, but her mind was so far from the fabric that nearly every stitch had to be ripped out and done again.

She'd almost given up hope when she heard the sound of the back door closing and the heavy footfalls of booted feet. With a quick glance in the mirror, she grabbed a bonnet and flew down the stairs, colliding abruptly with the solid wall of Tanner's broad chest.

"Oh, Tanner, I'm so sorry," she stammered as she backed up a step. "I guess I wasn't looking where I was going."

Tanner stared down into her face, her green eyes sparkling and her smooth cheeks flushed with excitement, and he felt his heart give an unfamiliar twist. He had the oddest sensation, as though the breath had been knocked from him, yet he knew the slight impact from her tiny form hadn't been nearly enough to do so.

"Good morning, Miss Garver," he said as he pulled the hat from his head. "I was just on my way up to call you. Are you ready for your lesson?"

"I've been ready!" she pronounced with an impish pout. "I didn't think you'd ever get here."

Tanner chuckled at her candid reply. He couldn't say why, but it pleased him to know she'd been looking forward to seeing him. "Rosa's got lunch all packed. We'll get the horses, and we'll be on our way."

Elise placed her bonnet on top of her head and began to tie the ribbons. She missed Tanner's upraised brow as he considered this latest outfit.

He'd grown accustomed to her odd color combinations, so the mint green blouse and red skirt looked completely normal to him. It was the hat that held his attention.

He wasn't certain he'd ever seen anything quite like it. It extended some six inches above her head and appeared to be covered with tiny clusters of fruit and bits of gauzy lace. It was pretty enough for a tea party, he supposed, but on the range? He had no doubt that during the course of their ride they'd be attacked by a flock of hungry birds. "Have you got something a little less, uh, fancy?" he asked tactfully.

Elise dropped her hands from the yellow ribbon and stared wide-eyed into his dark gaze. "Don't you like it?"

"Well, sure, I like it. It's just that I'm afraid uh, well, I'm afraid it might get messed up somehow."

She placed a hand on his arm and smiled warmly. "Aren't you sweet to be concerned. You mustn't worry, though. It's really quite sturdy." She gave the bow under her chin a final pat. "Shall we go?"

The sun was high overhead as the two of them crossed the yard toward the stables, with Elise practically running to keep up with Tanner's long strides. The now-familiar smell of freshly cut hay welcomed Elise as she stepped inside the cool shade of the building.

Elise watched as Tanner effortlessly saddled Miss Sadie. She couldn't help admiring his muscles straining beneath the fabric of his shirt as he lifted the heavy saddle into place. She leaned against the wooden stall to study him more carefully. Again she was reminded of how attractive he was. His ruggedly chiseled features and dark wavy hair were enough to make her weak-kneed.

"All set," he said as he turned to place the reins in Elise's hands. He must have felt her staring, because he quirked an inquisitive brow.

She felt herself blush to her toes. What would he think of such a bold woman? "Which horse will you be riding?" she asked, trying to divert attention from herself.

"Gypsy is tied up outside." He inclined his head toward Miss Sadie. "You ready?"

She nodded and Tanner lifted her high, placing her gently upon the pillow-topped saddle. Elise was relieved that he failed to mention the pillow, and even more relieved that he remembered to bring it.

He guided the horse out into the sunlight and around to the side of the stable where his horse was tethered.

Elise gasped her admiration. If James thought Elise and Miss Sadie were made for each other, so much more this horse and Tanner. She was an immense creature with a silky black coat that glistened in the late-morning sun. With her regal head held high, she stomped her hooves impatiently as she awaited her master. Becky was dwarfed standing beside it.

Tanner swung easily into the saddle. "Okay, Miss Garver, let's ride."

They took the horses out at a leisurely pace, stopping frequently to discuss some point of interest. Elise was fascinated by everything. "What is that long building over there?" she asked, pointing toward a structure well behind her father's house.

"That's the bunkhouse. For the hands."

"I never noticed it before. Is that where James lives?"

Tanner couldn't imagine why he felt a sharp jab of jealousy at the mention of James's name. His response was less than enthusiastic. "Yeah."

Elise didn't seem to notice. "It's lovely. Funny that I've never seen it before." She leaned forward in the saddle, looking from side to side, studying the panorama. "There's just so much to see. And it's all so beautiful."

She was truly enraptured by the ranch. The untamed beauty was breathtaking, but there was more. It was her father's. He'd carved out this prosperous business with his own two hands. Her heart swelled with pride. What a wonderful man he was.

Tanner was watching the unabashed delight on her face when a sudden jolt of inspiration struck. He reined his horse around and called back to her, "Follow me."

They rode due south through the swaying green grasses, slowly enough for Elise to stop and admire each bird or wildflower that caught her fancy. Becky would run off on her own to chase anything she could find and then reappear minutes later at their sides.

The wind picked up as they traveled, replacing the morning's fluffy white clouds with more substantial gray ones.

When they finally reached their destination, the crest of a tree-topped hill, Tanner reined his horse to a halt. He extended his arm before him, indicating that Elise should look.

She gasped with pure delight. Below her for as far as she could see, the valley was a sea of bright blue flowers waving merrily in the gusting winds. "Oh, Tanner!" she exclaimed without taking her eyes from the spectacle. "I've never seen anything so beautiful. What are they?"

"Texas bluebonnets." A wide grin spread across his face as he watched her enthusiastic response. He'd wanted to surprise her, and it was obvious he had done just that.

"They grow wild?"

"Yup. Come back every year."

She turned in the saddle to face him. "Do you suppose I could go down and pick some?"

"Sure. We'll come back on our way home." He checked the darkening sky. "We may have to cut our tour short today. Looks like a storm comin' in."

"And miss our picnic?" Elise sounded crushed. Her expression was so forlorn, he almost laughed.

Tanner glanced up at the threatening clouds. He knew the storm was imminent. He wanted to tell her the smartest thing they could do would be to ride back to the safety of the ranch, but one glance at the pleading look in her emerald eyes and he relented. "No, we'll have our picnic. And I know just the place. Come on."

He thought of the spring-filled pond back toward the house. There was even a cluster of trees they could sit under. It would be the perfect location. Elise would get her picnic, and he would have moved them closer to home before the storm hit.

Elise was obviously reluctant to leave the bluebonnets behind. With a heavy sigh, she tugged at Miss Sadie's reins, falling in behind Tanner. Becky obediently brought up the rear.

The sky grew more ominous by the minute. Thick black

clouds roiled overhead. The gusting wind had transformed into a steady gale. They were less than halfway to the picnic site, still three-quarters of an hour from the main house, when the first raindrops began to fall.

Tanner glanced toward Elise. He was relieved to see she didn't look fearful. Quite the opposite, in fact. She appeared to think the whole rain-splattered excursion was a lark. He noticed that her ridiculous fruit basket hat was doing an admirable job of keeping her dry. He supposed he ought to be thankful for small blessings.

He quickly revised his original plan. There would be no picnic today, that much was certain. But as long as the rain held slow, he'd head them back toward the house. With any luck, they'd beat the downpour.

No sooner had his brain registered the thought than the heavens opened up, and the rain began to come down in driving sheets.

"Ready to try a gallop?" he shouted to be heard above the wind.

Elise smiled brightly as raindrops coursed down her cheeks. "I'd love it."

"Use your legs and hold on tight!"

Tanner kicked his horse up and took off like a shot. Miss Sadie needed no encouragement to follow suit and they raced across the field side by side, with Becky keeping pace at their heels.

A bolt of lightning zigzagged across the sky, followed by a deafening crash. Miss Sadie balked slightly at the sound. Tanner knew they couldn't continue on toward the ranch now. It was too dangerous.

"This way," he shouted, signaling toward his left. He knew

of a small abandoned shack a few minutes to the west. They could stop there until the storm slacked off.

Minutes later the rain-drenched travelers thundered up to the cabin. Tanner dismounted quickly and lifted Elise from the saddle.

"Go on inside. You, too, Becky." Rivulets of water ran down his face as he spoke. "I'll take care of the horses and be in right behind you."

After tethering the horses securely inside the crude shelter behind the building, Tanner dashed to the door of the cabin and ducked inside.

Elise was waiting for him, standing in the center of the room, with her slender arms wrapped across her rain-soaked middle. She had removed her bonnet and he could see that her hair was drenched. So much for the fruity hat.

Becky was exploring, busily sniffing out the room, totally unconcerned about her own rain-plastered coat.

"I'm sorry about the mess," he apologized, surveying the dilapidated interior.

"It's dry," Elise said cheerfully, flashing him a shivery smile.

He couldn't help but grin. For a city kid, she sure had spunk.

"There's some wood in the fireplace. Let me get a fire started, and we'll see if we can get you dried out."

Elise nodded gratefully.

The well-seasoned wood caught fire instantly and Tanner had a crackling blaze going in no time. Once satisfied it would burn, he stood up to study their meager accommodations.

An old, scarred table was pushed up against the wall near the door. Beside it lay the fractured remains of the only chair in the room. No help there. A small cot along the far wall caught his attention and Tanner walked over to have a closer look. The mattress was patched and worn, but apparently clean.

He picked the mattress up, dusted it off, and carried it across the room, positioning it in front of the fire.

"Come sit here," he instructed Elise who stood watching him from the door.

She hesitated, nibbling her lower lip. Sitting on a mattress with a man was most unseemly. Aunt Claudia would certainly not approve of this. And Mrs. Rhoades's handbook was replete with warnings about just such an arrangement. Not that there was an alternative. She, too, had noticed the lack of seating in the room.

Tanner seemed to sense her reluctance. "You've got to sit down," he coaxed. "This is the spot where we'll have our picnic."

Elise didn't need a second invitation. It might be a bit unorthodox, but surely there was nothing improper about a picnic. She took the place he indicated on his left and faced the roaring fire. Almost immediately the warmth began to penetrate her rain-soaked skirt and shoes, and she breathed a sigh of pure contentment. She hadn't realized how cold she was.

Tanner retrieved his leather saddlebag from the doorway and joined her on the mattress. Sensing there was food to be had, Becky traipsed over and plopped down between them. She was not disappointed. Inside the bag, still dry, was the picnic lunch that Rosa had packed earlier. They ate without speaking, quickly demolishing the tasty food.

Outside, the storm raged on, but inside, a cheerful quiet pervaded with only the crackling flames to disturb the silence.

Becky gobbled her food in several greedy bites. Once filled, she wasted no time in finding a comfortable spot on the mattress to nap.

"She's a wonderful dog, Tanner. I've always wanted a pet," Elise said as she popped the last crumbs of her cookie into her mouth. "Have you had her long?"

"About four years. I took her in after her mother was killed. She'd been shot. Some greenhorn must have mistaken her for a wolf. Left old Becky all alone."

"How horrible. I bet that was especially painful for you, being an orphan yourself." She clapped a hand over her mouth as soon as the careless words escaped. "Oh, Tanner, I'm so sorry." Her eyes reflected her heartfelt remorse. "How rude of me to mention that."

Tanner shrugged. "You're right. In a way, Becky and I are a lot alike. Both of us were all alone and lucky enough to have someone take us in. If it weren't for Seth, I'm sure I'd be dead with the rest of my family."

"Don't even suggest such a thing."

"It's true. Seth saved my life that night." His dark eyes held hers. Something compelled him to continue. "We were coming West, a couple of families together, to make a new start. None of them made it. Indians attacked the wagons shortly after nightfall. The adults were sitting around the campfire, laughing and telling jokes. I was in the wagon with my kid brother. He had just fallen asleep when I heard the noise. I figured he was safe enough, so I slipped out for a minute to check things out."

Tanner stared into the leaping flames, his face a blank mask. "I crawled around to some bushes behind the campfire." He was silent for a moment, and his gaze dropped to his hands. When he spoke again, his voice was a low whisper. "What I saw was so horrible, I couldn't move. I just sat there. There wasn't any moon that night and things were dark so I couldn't make much out, but I could tell they were all dead. Every one of them."

Tears filled her eyes as Elise reached up and laid a cool hand against his cheek. "Don't, Tanner. Don't think about it anymore."

He stared at her in silence, the emotion in his dark eyes unreadable. After a long moment, he returned his gaze to the fire. "The Indians started screaming then, a noise that would make your skin crawl. The screams seemed to get me moving, and I remembered my brother.

"I crawled back through the bushes to the wagon. I remember it seemed to take forever. I was so scared, I could hardly move. That's when I saw the flames. Everything was burning." His voice broke. "Nobody could have survived it. Seth saw me and pulled me away before the Indians got me, too. He'd been riding by when he saw the fire and moved in for a closer look."

Tanner shook his head slightly, as if to clear his thoughts. His voice was stronger when he spoke again. "Your father is the finest man I've ever known." His eyes locked onto hers. "I owe him my life, and I'd do anything to protect him."

Elise attributed the fierceness of his oath to the emotion of the moment. She appreciated his loyalty to her father. He loved him as she did. And her father obviously loved

Tanner. She only wished that there was room in her father's heart for them both.

It seemed the most natural thing in the world when she inched over beside Tanner, her shoulder brushing his, and slipped her hand into his. "My father's a lucky man to have a friend like you."

Neither spoke again as they sat side by side, mesmerized by the dancing, golden flames. Elise could hear the rain falling against the roof. An occasional clap of thunder rattled the dilapidated building, but she felt safe from the violence of nature's fury. The warmth of the fire made her sleepy and her eyelids grew so heavy it became an effort just to keep them open. Perhaps, she thought, if I close them for a moment, the sinking spell will pass.

Tanner's thoughts were jumbled as he stared into the flames. He didn't know why he had poured out his heart to her, he'd kept his past closely guarded from others. After all these years, the memories were still too painful and the guilt he bore for his brother's death too fresh. Yet, he hadn't been able to stop the rush of words.

Interestingly enough, he felt better. He dropped a glance to the slender hand resting on his and smiled. He'd seen the tears in her eyes as she tried to comfort him. Tears of compassion.

Tanner's brow furrowed slightly. "Compassionate" didn't fit in with his initial appraisal of Elise. He had her pegged as a gold digger, pure and simple. A greedy opportunist out to collect her dying father's fortune to support her extravagant lifestyle.

He'd seen the evidence. Why, the price of her hats alone would put an average guy in the poorhouse. The thought of her hats brought a grimace to his face.

He didn't know how she and her aunt had been supporting themselves all these years, but the way he figured it, they had been biding their time, waiting for the news that Seth was dying. No doubt they knew the value of his holdings and were anxious to get their hands on it. The fact that Elise never communicated with her father until his illness seemed to validate his assumptions.

Tanner heard a yawn escape from Elise. He looked down at the top of her head, her mahogany tresses shimmering in the firelight. After spending time with her, it was becoming more and more difficult to imagine her as the enemy.

Suddenly, he knew he had to ask her, point blank, why she'd waited so long to see her father. What did she hope to gain by coming back after all these years. He had to know. Was she a conniving gold digger or a gentle woman of compassion? And he had to know now.

"Elise?" he began softly. "We need to talk." He turned slightly to see her face better. To his surprise, she didn't look up at him as he expected; instead, her head slumped against his chest. Closer inspection revealed that she'd fallen sound asleep.

Tanner grinned. Poor soul, she was no doubt exhausted by the afternoon's ordeal.

He settled back to allow himself the luxury of studying her at his leisure. Long, coal-black lashes fanned out against her creamy cheeks. Her lips, the color of roses, were parted slightly in slumber. A long, bronzed finger stole up to stroke her skin. It was just as soft as he had imagined.

He shifted slightly to wrap her in the protective circle

of his arms, and the scent of fresh flowers assailed him. As he cradled her more closely to his chest, Elise sighed contentedly in her sleep.

Tanner was aware of a change deep within himself that afternoon as he stared into the glowing embers. The barrier of suspicion coiled around his heart melted, leaving him free to listen to its direction.

Becky looked up at him from her place by the fire and cocked her ears. He chuckled. "Okay, okay," he whispered, "so you were right. I admit it, I fell for her. Now give it a rest."

◆

"Rosa! Where's Elise?" Seth demanded crossly from his bed. "I haven't seen her yet today."

Rosa placed his supper tray before him. "She and Tanner went out riding. I 'spect with this storm they had to stop someplace and wait it out. You'll just have to wait till tomorrow to visit with her."

"Tomorrow?" he wailed.

Rosa wagged a finger at him. "If you're looking for sympathy from me, you're barking up the wrong tree." She turned to walk from the room. "Far as I can see, it's your own fault you aren't with her." She stopped at the door to ask, "Hasn't this dying business gone far enough?"

Seth shrugged helplessly. "What choice do I have?"

"How about the truth?"

"We've been through this before," Seth said with a sigh of resignation. "The truth wouldn't get Elise here. You yourself admitted that Claudia would settle for nothing less than death."

Rosa stalked back over to the bed. "*Sí,* that's true, Seth.

But the child's here, now. Must we continue with the lie?"

"She wouldn't stay, Rosa. If she knew the truth, that I'm as healthy as she is, she'd run back to Boston so fast, it would make my head spin."

"Oh Seth, be reasonable. She's your daughter."

Seth's eyes met Rosa's. "I haven't been completely honest with you. I never told you why Elise stayed in Boston."

"Certainly you did. You thought Claudia was better equipped to raise a young lady."

He shook his head. "The truth is, I wanted her back. She hadn't been gone a month when I realized my mistake." His voice was a whisper. "A father should raise his own daughter."

He stared past Rosa for a moment before he continued, "Anyway, I went to Boston to tell Claudia I wanted Elise to come home. Claudia wouldn't hear of it. She told me I was selfish, and that if I was any kind of a father at all, I'd think of the child's well-being.

"I foolishly agreed to give her a year. No longer." He raked his fingers through his hair. "With the war and all, the year stretched to two, then three. I couldn't have risked her life, trying to travel across the states, so I waited longer, till things settled down.

"Finally, I went back to Boston. Elise was nearly eight by then. I was desperate to bring her home. I wasn't going to take 'no' for an answer." Seth fell silent.

"Well, go on." Rosa urged, "Did you see the child? Why didn't you bring her home?"

"I got there late in the morning and, Elise had already gone to school. That's when Claudia told me."

"Told you what, Seth? You're not making a lick of sense."

"She told me Elise hated me. She said Elise blamed me for the death of her mother." His voice wavered. "Claudia said the very thought of me gave the child nightmares." He raised pain-filled eyes to Rosa. "I couldn't take her then."

"You believed her?" Rosa was incredulous. "You believed the old crab?"

"I had to. She had nothing to gain by keeping Elise. Why would she lie?"

Rosa was quiet for a moment as she sorted through what she had heard. "But Seth," she said finally, "Elise came to you. Doesn't that mean anything?"

He shook his head. "Claudia made it clear that Elise was coming only out of her sense of duty. Fulfilling a dying man's request. Nothing more."

"I for one don't believe it. Elise is a lovely young woman. I can't imagine her hating anyone."

Seth nodded his agreement.

"Ask her. Ask her how she feels."

"I can't. Claudia made me agree not to talk about it. She said Elise would come only on the condition that I would not discuss our relationship. Not one word."

Rosa threw her hands up in disgust. "Then what do we do? Continue this ridiculous pretending? And for how long?"

"For as long as it takes to make her love me."

"And just how do you propose to do that?"

"Slowly, little by little. We're strangers now and I hardly know what to say to her. So I'm going real slow. We'll start out with short visits in the afternoon, like we're doing now. I don't want to rush her. When I notice she's enjoying our time together, then I'll get better, you know, healthier, so that I can have meals with her and spend more time together."

He looked over to see Rosa shaking her head in disapproval. "This is my only chance, Rosa. If I offend her and she leaves, I may never see her again."

nine

Elise stood just inside her bedroom door, her ears trained on the sound of familiar booted feet traveling across the wooden floors toward the back of the house. She breathed a sigh of relief a moment later when she heard the hinges of the back door squeak as it swung open and closed.

She was much later than usual for breakfast this morning and her stomach growled a complaint. She paid it no heed. A little hunger was a small price to pay for the assurance of not facing Tanner this morning. After her unfortunate behavior yesterday, she doubted she'd ever have the courage to face him again.

As a precaution, she tiptoed ever so carefully across the hall and began a silent descent of the stairs, her ears alert for any sound of his return.

She smiled triumphantly as she stepped from the last stair, having successfully made it down without a sound. Her eyes remained on her feet as she rounded the corner toward the kitchen. Elise was so intent upon stealth, she failed to notice the man, dressed in black, leaning negligently against the kitchen door frame, until she was practically upon him.

"Oh, Tanner!" she cried, clapping a hand over her heart, "I thought I heard you leave; uh, what I mean is I didn't think you'd still be here."

"Good morning to you, too," he drawled, a lazy grin on his face. "You weren't thinking to avoid me this morning, were you?"

Elise dropped her gaze. She felt the heat of the blush on her cheeks as she replied, "No, not exactly." It was true. The plan was to avoid him for the rest of her life.

"Good." His lips pulled into a roguish smile. "You and I have some unfinished business to attend to this morning."

"We do?" Elise barely recognized the squeak as her own voice.

He nodded solemnly. "Matter of honor, actually."

Elise didn't think it was possible to blush any harder. Her face felt so hot that at any moment she expected to smell smoke. Honor could mean only one thing. He was referring to yesterday's fiasco.

Tanner appeared unmoved by her plight. He took her elbow and propelled her through the back door to the yard where Gypsy was waiting.

"Are we going somewhere?" Elise managed a tremulous smile.

He nodded.

"I'll run get my hat while you saddle Miss Sadie for me." *Or perhaps just keep on running,* she thought grimly.

Tanner tightened his grip on her arm. "We won't be gone long, so you don't need a hat, and since I'm running short on time, you can ride with me."

He swung up easily behind the saddle, then motioned for Elise to give him her hands. She did so obediently and he scooped her up, settling her on the saddle in front of him.

Elise did her best to remain rigid, so that her shoulder wouldn't come in contact with Tanner's broad chest. She wouldn't make the same mistake as yesterday.

Just thinking about it now was as embarrassing as it was

yesterday when she awakened in his arms. True, it felt wonderful, cradled against his strong chest, the fresh, clean scent of him surrounding her. And, yes, he had been the perfect gentlemen, releasing her as soon as she was awake. But just the same, it was no way for a proper young lady to act.

She had tried to apologize well over a hundred times. Elise swallowed hard. Evidently, it hadn't been enough. Unfinished business could mean only one thing. He meant to tell her just what he thought of such a brazen woman. Of course, it was no less than she deserved. Aunt Claudia had been right—bad blood would tell.

Elise tried to look on the bright side. The fact that he was taking her away from the house to scold her meant that her father would not hear. She couldn't bear to think that he would find out about her impropriety. He would never love her then.

Gypsy's long legs ate up the range as she galloped into the breeze. Elise's valiant struggle to remain upright made the ride most uncomfortable.

Tanner seemed to sense her discomfort. He leaned forward to whisper, "It's all right, Miss Garver, you can lean against me."

She sank gratefully against him, his two strong arms flanking her sides. As her cheek pressed against his crisp cotton shirt, Elise closed her eyes and smiled to herself. This time snuggled beside him somehow made the coming punishment well-worth it.

Elise did not know how far they had traveled before Gypsy climbed a rise and Tanner reined her to a halt. "Here we are," he announced.

And here it comes, Elise added silently. She reluctantly

raised her head from its resting place on his chest and stared up expectantly into his dark eyes.

"Well, go on." His deep voice held a smile. "Get busy."

"Busy?" Elise was totally perplexed.

"Didn't you say you wanted to pick bluebonnets?"

Elise's green eyes opened wide. Slowly she turned away from him to gaze out across the field of blue. "Oh, Tanner!" she squealed in delight as she slid from the horse and raced out into the sea of bluebonnets.

Tanner remained atop Gypsy to watch Elise gambol through the flowers. The sunlight danced off her hair and he was glad he hadn't given her time to find a bonnet.

He resisted a twinge of guilt over the high-handed way he got her out here this morning. True, he didn't have much time, but he certainly could have waited the short time it would have taken to saddle Miss Sadie. The fact was, he didn't want Elise to ride her own horse. He wanted her next to him, in his arms, just as she had been the day before.

He leaned forward atop Gypsy to watch her bend gracefully to pluck another bluebonnet. He was relieved to see she was in good spirits after yesterday's adventure. The way she had kept apologizing and blushing, he was afraid she'd never speak to him again.

He dismounted as she approached, her face wreathed in smiles. "Oh look, Tanner," she held up her bouquet for his inspection. "Aren't they lovely?"

His eyes never left her face. "Very."

Elise's smile faded as she broached the subject she dreaded. "Was there some other reason you wanted to see me this morning?"

"No." Tanner shrugged. "Should there be?"

She shook her head, blushing furiously in spite of herself.

Suddenly, he seemed to understand. "This is about yesterday, isn't it? Did you think I was angry with you? That you did something wrong?"

She bit her bottom lip and nodded. "I fell asleep on you," came her strangled confession.

He struggled not to smile at the memory. "Guess it does sound kinda incriminating, but it was completely innocent. It's just one of those things that sounds bad when you try to explain it."

"But—"

"No, Elise," Tanner cut her off before she could continue, "you did nothing wrong. The fact is, the blame is mine that we were there in the first place. Mine and the storm's." He took her hands in his. "You were the picture of propriety."

Her face brightened with his words.

"I brought you here today only because I promised you could pick flowers. You looked so disappointed when we left yesterday." He took her chin in his hand and tilted her face to his. "I brought you back because I love to see you smile."

Tears welled in Elise's eyes. "You know, this is one of the nicest things anyone has ever done for me." She continued earnestly, "Next to Rosa, you must be the kindest person I know."

"Rosa, huh?" he teased.

She gave a solemn nod. "Do you know the entire time I've been here, she's never once mentioned my awful taste in colors or the fact that my behavior frequently falls short of proper." Elise's voice was awed as she said, "I think she really cares for me. She even taught me how to become a Christian." Concern suddenly marred her brow. "Tanner, are you a Christian?"

He nodded.

"Are you sure? I mean, there's more to becoming a Christian than just attending church. You have to make a personal decision to accept Jesus as your Savior."

Tanner laughed. "I can tell Rosa's been after you, and yes, I am absolutely certain that I am a Christian."

"I'm so glad." Elise sighed contentedly. The matter resolved, and her heart lighter, she turned back toward the field of flowers. "It's so lovely; I believe I could stay here for hours."

"Not today, I'm afraid. I've got to get back. The boys are waiting on me for the branding." He hated to see her bright smile fade. "Tell you what. We'll come back another time. For a picnic."

Elise beamed. "I'll hold you to it. Matter of honor."

Tanner put his foot into the stirrup and climbed onto Gypsy, then leaned over to pick up Elise. He gently placed her before him, careful not to crush her flowers.

She turned slightly, so she could look up into his face. "Thank y—" The words caught in her throat when she realized his handsome face was just inches from hers. All rational thought fled as she stared up into his dark eyes.

It took sheer strength of will to drag her eyes away. She stared down at the bouquet on her lap. "Thank you, Tanner. For everything."

His response was a husky whisper. "No, Miss Garver, thank *you*."

Elise settled comfortably against his chest to make the trip home.

ten

"Elise, *querida*, I've got a great idea," Rosa said.

Elise dropped the heavy basket of wet laundry on the ground and with the back of her hand, wiped the beads of perspiration from her forehead.

"I hope it doesn't involve any more cleaning," she laughed weakly.

"Oh, no, much better," Rosa assured her as she joined Elise at the basket and the women began to hang out the clothes on the line. "We're going swimming."

Elise wasn't sure she had heard correctly. "Swimming?" she repeated.

"*Sí*." Rosa nodded enthusiastically.

"No, Rosa, I don't think so." Elise shook her head.

"Sure, we will. It's really out here today and we've worked up a sweat. A swim is just what we need to cool off."

"No, no, I don't think so. I'll have to pass," Elise persisted. "Aunt Claudia has always insisted that swimming isn't proper." She paused, trying to find a more solid argument. "And besides, I don't have a thing to wear."

Rosa laughed mischievously. "Oh, yes you do."

Elise was still protesting an hour later when Rosa pulled the buggy to a stop under a stand of oaks. She hopped down from the buggy and followed Rosa through the copse of trees, toward the pond. "But I don't even know how to swim."

"That's fine, honey," Rosa dismissed her argument with a wave of her hand. "The water's pretty shallow for swimming, anyway."

They reached a pile of large rocks that stood in a semi-circle in front the pond. Elise gasped as Rosa casually slipped off her dress and folded it neatly on top of the rocks, before proceeding around the pile and into the water wearing only her camisole and petticoat.

"Rosa!" she exclaimed in true horror. "What if someone should see you?"

"Who's gonna see me out here? Nobody's around except you and me and old Seth up at the house, and he sure can't see this far. I don't expect the boys back from branding for at least another day."

"Oh," Elise said in a very small voice. She had hoped they'd be back sooner. In the week since she and Tanner had taken refuge from the storm in the old abandoned shack, she'd barely seen him, much less talked to him. She'd never had a friend like him, and she found she missed him very much.

"The water feels wonderful," Rosa cajoled as she paddled around. "It's so cool and refreshing."

Elise's thoughts whirled back to the present dilemma. Rosa was a hard woman to refuse. But then, what harm could there be in a little wading, she asked herself. Claudia never actually expressed her disapproval of wading; it was swimming she considered immoral. Since her own conscience didn't convict her of any wrongdoing, perhaps she could give it a try. Besides, she rationalized, who would ever know?

After removing her shoes and stockings, she took a

tentative step toward the pond and dipped her toe into the crystal-clear water. It *was* refreshingly cool, just as Rosa had said. Somewhat heartened, Elise stepped in, holding her skirts above the ankle-deep water.

"You might as well take the skirt off," Rosa called from the middle of the pond where she floated on her back. "It's just gonna get wet, and we'll have more laundry to do."

Elise groaned. That argument was highly effective in light of the grueling morning they had spent washing clothes.

"You win," she said with a sigh of resignation. She climbed out of the water and slowly removed her skirt and blouse. The layers of fabric that comprised her camisole and petticoat provided more than modest coverage, but she couldn't help feeling a bit sheepish about being outdoors in her undergarments. She glanced nervously from side to side as she folded her clothes and added them to the pile with Rosa's.

Satisfied that she and Rosa were alone, she scampered into the pond, walking out to where the water came up to her waist. A sudden movement from behind caught her eye and before she could react, Rosa popped up from under the water and drenched her with a splash.

Elise laughed and retaliated with a splash and the battle was on.

≥∞

Tanner pushed his hat back off his forehead and mopped the perspiration from his brow. "What a scorcher, Becky. I don't remember the heat ever being this bad in April."

Becky flopped down at the feet of his horse, her tongue

lolling from her mouth.

"Tell you what. We've got time for a quick swim before we ride in to surprise the women. Why don't we stop at the spring?"

Becky was on her feet in an instant, running around the horse and yapping excitedly. Tanner grinned as the threesome loped through the grass toward the pond. He couldn't wait to see the look on Miss Garver's face when he showed up for dinner tonight.

He hadn't realized how much he would miss her while he was tied up with the spring branding. He'd actually been counting the hours till he could get back to see her. He could hardly wait for tonight.

Tanner was still a long way off when he spotted the familiar black buggy parked under the trees. His brows furrowed slightly. "Now what do you suppose Rosa's doing out here in the middle of the day?"

He kicked up the horse to a gallop, sending clods of dirt flying behind him as he covered the distance in record time. Concern replaced curiosity when he pulled up beside the buggy and heard the screams. His heart lurched sickeningly within his chest. Somebody had Rosa! Tanner sprang from the saddle, hitting the ground at a dead run. He kept low, dodging from tree to tree, finally taking cover behind the rock pile.

Blood hammered in his brain as he checked his gun. Who would be on Garver land? Somebody must have been watching the place to know the men were gone. But why was Rosa out here, away from the house? He looked up suddenly. He had a gut feeling something was wrong. The screams had stopped. He didn't want to think of what had happened.

Tanner cocked his gun and stood, legs braced, ready to open fire, when he noticed the pile of neatly folded clothes. At that same moment, a high-pitched squeal pierced the air, followed by a riotous burst of giggles. Elise. Elise and Rosa. Tanner slumped against the rocks with relief. They weren't hurt. From the sound of things, they were playing.

Becky started toward the pond at the sound of familiar voices. Tanner reached out and grabbed her, crouching down beside her. "Not so fast," he whispered. "I owe them a good scare."

He waited for a lull in the giggling before getting to his feet. In a loud voice he called, "Here we are, Becky, ready to go swimming. Sure hope the water's cold. Won't take me but just a second to get these clothes off."

Piercing screams rent the air. Tanner chuckled at his success.

"Tanner?" Rosa's voice was unsteady. "Is that you?"

Tanner stayed behind the rock, his voice the picture of innocence. "Rosa? What are you doing out here?"

"Stay where you are!" she warned. "Better yet, why don't you walk on over to the buggy. . .it's parked under the trees. . .and wait. Elise and I need to get our clothes."

"Your clothes?" Tanner feigned shock. "Do you mean to tell me that you ladies have been skinny dipping?"

"Never mind that, Mr. Smarty. Just get on over to the buggy," Rosa snapped. "And be quick about it."

Tanner took his time sauntering over to the buggy, careful not to look back toward the water. He leaned against it to wait, his arms folded over his chest, his ankles crossed.

Minutes later, the women emerged through the trees. Any

thought he had had of teasing them died as he spotted Elise. Her face was the picture of mortification and she refused to look at him, choosing instead to study the ground.

"Thought I'd surprise you by coming in early. Looks like I was real successful." He winked at Rosa, but Elise's gaze remained downcast. "Would you like an escort back to the house?"

Rosa took one look at Elise and shook her head. "No, I think we'll go on ahead. You and Becky can clean up here, and we'll see you for dinner."

"Sounds fair. See you then."

❧

"Why don't you young people carry yourselves out to the front porch, while I clean up these dishes?" Rosa asked, picking up several plates from the table.

Elise, who'd been conspicuously quiet all evening, spoke up quickly, "Oh, no, I'd like to help."

"Wouldn't hear of it, *querida.*" She dismissed her offer with a wave of her hand. "There's too little here for the two of us. Besides," she glanced meaningfully toward Tanner, "there's a cool breeze out there tonight and a beautiful full moon. You haven't lived till you've seen a Texas moon."

"But. . . ."

"Rosa's right," Tanner's deep voice chimed in. "You haven't really seen Texas until you've sat out on the porch under a full moon." He walked over to stand behind her chair. "Rosa can join us when she's finished."

Seeing the futility of further argument, Elise conceded, reluctantly following Tanner's tall frame down the hall and out through the front door with Becky close on her heels. After this afternoon's humiliation at the pond, he was the very last person with whom she wanted to be alone.

She sat stiffly in one of the high-back rocking chairs, her hands folded primly in her lap. Tanner took the seat beside her, crossing his long legs at the ankles. For a long time, neither spoke.

"Tanner?"

"Miss Garver?"

They each chose the exact same moment to break the silence. Elise giggled in spite of herself. "Go ahead."

Tanner shook his dark head. "You first."

"I. . .I wanted to apologize about this afternoon."

"For what?" Tanner was obviously baffled.

Elise was glad for the cover of darkness to shroud her flaming cheeks. "I behaved badly, I'm afraid." She dropped her gaze to her lap and nibbled the corner of her lip. "I knew swimming, especially in my uh, well um, especially dressed the way I was, was completely improper." She raised her eyes to his. "I just hope you won't judge me too harshly."

"Judge you for swimming?" Tanner's voice was incredulous.

Elise nodded. "You said it yourself. We were skinny dipping." She hung her head and mused aloud. "Why is it do you suppose that someone who spends as much time studying proper behavior as I do, has so much trouble applying it? It seems I'm continually entrenched in compromising situations."

Tanner suppressed a laugh. "Have you struggled with this problem long?"

"No." She frowned, trying to pinpoint the exact time the problem began. "Just since I arrived in Texas."

Tanner grinned unsympathetically. "Maybe it's the

climate."

"My father will be so ashamed."

Tanner was confused. "Now wait a minute. How will he find out? Do you think I'm going to tell your father?"

Elise nodded again. "Well, yes, aren't you? I mean, you two are the best of friends, and I'm sure you discuss everything. I know you carry a strong influence with him."

Tanner captured her hands in his. "Miss Garver, 'round here folks don't go in big for swimming clothes. Fact is, swimming in your underwear is normal. Since it was just you and Rosa that saw each other, I can't find a thing for you to be ashamed of. I was just teasing you when I said that about skinny dipping."

"You were?" Her voice was hopeful. "You mean you're not offended? You won't mention it to my father?"

Tanner nodded, a smile playing at the corner of his mouth. "I think this falls under the category of one of those things that sounds bad when you try to explain it."

"Oh, Tanner!" She squeezed his hands that still held hers. "I'm so glad. I was afraid I'd ruined everything. I guess I'm not doing a very good job as a new Christian."

"Speaking as an old Christian, I think you're doing just fine."

Elise sighed her relief. "I'm happy you think so." She paused to study his handsome face. "You've been a Christian a while, so you must already know what it's like to have God answer your prayers."

"Well, uh sorta," he hedged.

She tilted her head to one side in question.

"Honestly, I'm not too big on praying," he admitted sheepishly.

She gave his hand a comforting pat. "Don't feel bad. You can start fresh with me. Rosa has me reading the book of John. She says it's a great place for new Christians to start." Her voice became more animated with her enthusiasm. "Maybe we could read the same chapters and discuss them." She stopped herself in midsentence. "You do have a Bible, don't you?"

"Yeah."

"Good. Read the first two chapters and if you have time tomorrow, maybe we can discuss what we've read."

Tanner grinned. "I'll try." He paused for a moment before adding, "Say, I've got to go into town tomorrow for a few supplies. Why don't you ride in with me. We can talk then."

With enthusiastic abandon, Elise threw her arms around his neck and hugged him tightly. "It sounds wonderful. I can't wait." She suddenly realized what she was doing and quickly withdrew her arms. She cleared her throat self-consciously and stood up, walking over to the porch railing. "The sky is so lovely in Texas," she said in an obvious attempt to change the subject. "I don't think I've ever seen so many stars."

Tanner strode over to join her. "It's a beautiful clear, night."

Elise sighed wistfully. "It's so peaceful and lovely here. Heavenly, don't you think?"

Tanner ignored the sky, choosing instead to move closer, concentrating his full attention on her upturned face. The light from inside the house cast a golden glow on her delicate features. An errant breeze carried with it her sweet scent of flowers, and he was reminded of how soft her skin felt to his touch. "Definitely heavenly." His whispered words were almost a caress.

Elise startled at the proximity of his voice; she hadn't heard him move so close. She glanced hesitantly in his direction and their eyes met. Elise's heart hammered wildly within her chest as Tanner placed his hands on her shoulders, gently turning her toward him. He brushed a wispy strand of hair from her face. "Elise," he whispered huskily, "I..."

The hinges of the front door creaked. "See now, I told you it wouldn't take long—" Rosa began as she stepped onto the porch. "Oh!" she exclaimed as she saw the two of them. "Looks like you were planning on a little more time alone."

Tanner dropped his hands to his sides, and Elise backed away guiltily. "No, Rosa, come on out. We were just about to say good night. Isn't that right, Tanner?"

"Something like that," he answered wryly.

"Anyway, it's getting late. I think I'll go on in and get a good night's rest before tomorrow's trip into town." Elise flashed a nervous smile over her shoulder before ducking through the front doorway. "Good night. See you both in the morning," she called. "And Tanner, don't forget your assignment."

Rosa was puzzled. "What assignment is that, Tanner?"

"Hmmmmm?"

She caught sight of the silly grin on his face as he stared after Elise and she shook her head in disbelief. "Tanner and Elise? I'm seeing it, and I still don't believe it."

eleven

"Elise, have you got my list?" Rosa asked.

Elise patted the pocket of her skirt. "Right here."

"Good enough." Rosa stepped back from the wagon. "Be careful, you two. And have fun."

Tanner nodded and slapped the reins, directing the horses toward the town.

The late-April morning was bright with promise. Golden sunlight glittered magically on the crystalline dewdrops carpeting the endless fields. Elise settled back on the bench, content for a time to sit quietly at Tanner's side, watching with interest as he handled the horses. "Is it proper for a woman to drive a team?" she blurted out at last.

Tanner's teeth flashed in a grin. "Sure, it's proper. Downright necessary for Texans." His dark eyes sparkled. "You wanna try?"

Elise's eyes grew wide. "Me? Really?"

Tanner chuckled at her enthusiasm over the simplest things. "Really." He slid over closer to her on the bench and placed the reins in her hands, wrapping his hands around hers to steady them.

"The horses are trained to respond to your commands and the tension you keep in the reins," he began the instruction. "It's similar to how you handle Miss Sadie."

With her hands clasped in his, Elise had difficulty concentrating on what he was saying. His clean, masculine scent and handsome face captured her attention. She actually felt breathless.

"I think you'll be more successful if you keep your eyes on the road."

Elise jerked her eyes from his face to the road in front of her. She hadn't meant to stare, and she certainly hadn't meant to get caught. She chewed her lower lip in mortification. The man had the most peculiar effect on her senses.

"I'm disappointed in you, Miss Garver," Tanner said, breaking the embarrassed silence as the wagon rattled down the dirt road. "You haven't asked me about my assignment."

Elise's eyes lit with delight. "Tanner, you *did* read the chapters from John!" Having her hands on the reins restrained her from hugging him. "I'm so glad. I want you to tell me which verse was your favorite. But first, I must ask a favor of you."

He raised his brow.

"Would you please call me Elise?"

"Elise." Tanner repeated her name softly before favoring her with a warm smile. "I think I can handle that."

Elise felt her heart give an inexplicable jump. Her name had never sounded that good coming from anyone else's lips. "Uh, yes, well then," she fumbled around, trying to remember what it was she was saying, "which verse did you like best?"

"I liked the part where it says anybody can be a child of God, just by believing in Jesus."

Elise handed him back the reins so she could pull her Bible out of the basket at her feet. She flipped through the pages to the book of John and skimmed the the first chapter. "Here it is, verse twelve: "But as many as received him, to them gave he power to become the sons of God, even to them that believe on his name." She looked over at Tanner. "That's mine, too. What a wonderful promise. It makes us part of a family."

"Family?" He shook his dark head. "I never thought of it that way before. I just like it 'cuz it shows how simple it is to be saved."

"That's true, of course, but there's so much more. That verse is a promise. I think it's a special promise to people like you and me who have lost our family or have been separated from them. It assures us that even in the loneliest times, we belong to God. We're His family, and He cares for us. The best part is that because we are His children, He'll answer our prayers."

Tanner shoved his hat back as he studied her for a moment. "You know, you amaze me. For someone who's just become a Christian, you're heads above me already."

She shook her head. "You're being too hard on yourself."

"No, I mean it. I was saved a long time ago and haven't honestly given God much thought since then."

"Why not?"

He shrugged his broad shoulders. "I don't know. I guess I didn't figure I needed to. Fact is, I've been handling things pretty.well without God."

Their discussion came to an abrupt halt as Tanner pulled the wagon up in front of the store. Elise was disappointed to see it end.

"Where to first?" she asked after Tanner secured the team and lifted her to the ground.

"I've got to head over to the livery for some supplies. Why don't you go on into the general store and pick up the things on Rosa's list. I'll probably finish first, so I'll be back here to meet you."

Before proceeding into the store, Elise lingered on the sidewalk for a moment to watch him cross the street. The shopkeeper nodded politely to acknowledge her presence then returned his attention to his customer.

Elise was mesmerized by the sights and smells of the store. Unlike the specialty shops of Boston, this store seemed to carry an endless range of products. She wandered to each corner, stopping to study the rows of canned goods or to finger the bolts of fabric.

"Can I help you, ma'am?"

Elise smiled up at the shopkeeper. "Yes, please. I've got a list here, from Rosa Viegas."

He grinned. "You must be Seth's daughter. I can tell by them green eyes. I heard tell you were coming. Fact is, I got a letter here for you. From Boston, I think."

"A letter?" Elise was distracted as the door swung open to admit Tanner.

"Howdy, Mr. Dalton." The shopkeeper stepped forward to shake Tanner's hand. "How's things at the ranch?"

"Just fine, Nathan. Herd's looking better than ever this year."

"Glad to hear it. Anything I can get for you today?"

Tanner shook his head. "Nothing for me, thanks. Miss Garver's got the list." Tanner's gaze strayed over to Elise and fell on her hat. "Say, wait, there is one thing." He looked back at Nathan. "What have you got in the way of hats?"

"Got a new box in last week." He pointed toward the

front of the store. "They're over there, by the window. Help yourself."

Tanner took Elise's arm, guiding her through the cluttered aisles and toward the window. "Come on, we're going to find you a decent...," his gaze rested on her bonnet, this one boasting an enormous pink satin bow and a tuft of pheasant feathers, "uh, I mean a sturdy hat to wear while you're riding."

He located the boxes and began rummaging through the contents, finally selecting a plain, black felt hat similar to his own. He held it up for her inspection. "What about something like this?"

Elise doubted seriously that Mrs. Rhoades would approve. "I don't know, Tanner," she said, her hesitant smile revealing her misgivings. "It looks awfully masculine, don't you think?"

Tanner grinned as he studied the bundle of femininity before him. "Trust me, that shouldn't be a problem on you."

Elise obediently removed her bonnet and placed the black hat on her head. "Well?"

Tanner chuckled. "Let's get it at the correct angle." He stood in front of her, tilting the hat slightly forward. She stared up at him, waiting patiently for him to finish the adjustments.

He smiled with satisfaction as he gave it a final quick pat. Slowly his dark gaze traveled down to meet hers. His smile suddenly melted and the look in his eyes became serious. Elise was powerless to look away, totally enchanted by the ebony depths. Ever so slowly, he lowered his head toward hers. Instinctively, she slanted her head backwards and her eyes fluttered closed.

His lips gently brushed hers, sending shock waves through

her body. The kiss lasted only a fraction of a second, yet it rendered Elise breathless. Tanner, too, seemed shaken by the brief contact.

"Does that mean it looks all right?" Elise asked with an unsteady voice.

"What? Oh yeah, the hat." Tanner stepped back to consider her. "Just perfect."

"This everything, Mr. Dalton?" Nathan called from the counter.

Tanner pointed to the hat on Elise's head. "We'll take this, too."

They were loaded in the wagon, with the packages neatly stowed away when Nathan popped out from the store, waving an envelope. "I nearly forgot your letter, Miss Garver!" He handed it up to her. "Regards to your father and Rosa."

"Thank you." Elise tucked the letter into the basket along with the Bible. "Goodbye."

&

"So what'd you think of Crossroads?" Tanner asked as he headed the wagon home.

"It's wonderful." Elise saw the look of amused disbelief on his face. "No, really, I mean it. There's such a comfortable feeling here in Crossroads, and Texas, too. Almost like I belong here."

Tanner's eyes were warm as they held hers. "Maybe you do."

Elise shook her head sadly. "If only that were true. But there's Boston and Aunt Claudia and. . .Oh! I almost forgot her letter. I suppose I ought to see what she has to say."

She plucked the envelope from the basket and settled back against the bench to read.

Dear Elise,

It was evident from the tone of your letter that you are enjoying your visit to Texas. I must remind you that your obligations lie here in Boston. There's Percival to consider; he's quite anxious to be married.

By the time this letter reaches you, I will be on my way to join you in Texas. It is time for you to return to Boston to resume your duties, and I have grave misgivings about allowing you to travel alone.

Percival will be accompanying me. He is most interested in seeing Texas and your father's holdings.

Elise couldn't believe her eyes. This couldn't be happening. Aunt Claudia coming to bring her home? Her heart twisted in her chest. She couldn't leave now. She hadn't earned her father's love. And what about Tanner? She read the letter again, hoping that somehow she was mistaken.

"Oh, no," Elise wailed dismally and slumped against the bench as the words of the letter sank in.

Tanner's brows furrowed with concern. "What's the matter, Elise? Is something wrong with your aunt?"

"No. She's fine," Elise replied gloomily. "In fact, she's coming here."

"To Texas?"

Elise nodded her dismay. "That's not the worst of it. She's bringing my fiancé."

Tanner reined the horses to an abrupt halt. "Your *what?*"

Elise continued to stare at the letter in her hands. "My fiancé."

Tanner's voice was dangerously calm as he asked. "You're engaged?"

"Uh-huh."

"You never mentioned you're going to be married."

Something in his tone of voice alerted Elise to his displeasure. She glanced up from the paper to see the dark fury in his eyes, and she blanched when she realized he was angry with her. "I guess I forgot." She tried to laugh, but the sound was more of a nervous squeak.

"You forgot?" Tanner's voice remained quiet. . .deadly quiet.

"That sounds silly I suppose. I mean, one shouldn't forget something as important as that, but you see," Elise stammered, "it happened so suddenly, just before I left to come here, actually, and with everything else that's happened, it just slipped my mind." She gave a helpless shrug of her shoulders. "It's not like it seems—"

Tanner raised a hand to silence her. "It's all becoming very clear to me." A muscle in his cheek twitched as he struggled to control his anger. "I've been such a fool. You really are here because you want something from your father. Guess you figure that since you're his daughter you deserve it."

Elise nodded her head very slowly. After all, what Tanner said was true, to a point. She had come to Texas to gain something from her father—His love.

"You've been waiting all this time to get what you think is coming to you, and now that Seth is sick you've decided it's time to collect."

Elise stared at him in wide-eyed amazement. He didn't understand her motivation, but he did seem to see through her plan. "Well, yes, that's true I guess, but it's not what you think. . ."

Tanner wouldn't let her finish. "Just how long have you been planning this little scheme?"

Elise flushed scarlet at his choice of words. Scheme. Hadn't her own heart warned her that scheming for her father's affection was wrong.

"I didn't want to scheme." She wrung her hands as she spoke. How humiliating to have to explain how naive she'd been, that she had actually believed her father loved her. "I never knew I'd need to. But after I got here and saw the situation for myself. . . ."

Tanner laughed bitterly at the sight of her red-stained cheeks, seeing them as further proof of her guilt. "What an idiot I've been," he berated himself. "I actually believed you cared for me."

"But I do care for you." Elise's green eyes glittered with tears as she blurted out, "Don't you see, Tanner? I. . .I love you."

"You love me?" Tanner's face grew white with fury. "Enough of this game, Miss Garver," he shouted. "You're engaged! It's your father you're after. I'm just a convenient way to get to him. A strong influence is the way you put it, I believe." He turned an accusing glare on her, daring her to contradict him. "Go ahead. Tell me I'm not just a part of your plan."

"Maybe at first," Elise admitted reluctantly, "but if you'll just let me explain—"

"Spare me your explanations, Miss Garver," he gritted

out. "If you're very quiet, maybe I'll forget you're here and allow you to ride back to the ranch."

"But—"

"It's a long walk." Tanner growled the warning.

Elise lowered her head, accepting defeat. They rode home in silence.

twelve

Elise paused at her father's door and rested her cheek against the cool, oak panel. Her heart ached within her. She'd never felt so defeated in her life.

It was over. Her one chance to earn her father's love was gone. Aunt Claudia was on her way to whisk Elise back to her responsibilities in Boston, away from her father forever.

She had failed. Her vow to have her father's love before she left would go unfulfilled. Hot tears of disappointment welled up in her eyes. She'd counted on more time. She needed more time. She knew now that love couldn't be rushed.

Except in my own case, she amended with a sad little sigh. A lone tear strayed down her cheek as Tanner's face flashed through her memory. It was true. She was in love with Tanner. Elise shook her head with dismay. Her own heart hadn't been slow. In the course of a few short weeks, it found its deepest desire in the form of a tall, dark cowboy. And she wasn't even looking!

A second tear trailed the first. How could things have gotten so bad? The two men she loved didn't love her back. Her father was polite enough, of course, but it was time to face the truth. Her father didn't want or need her. She was here as a loose end, nothing more.

And Tanner hated her. Elise winced at the memory of this afternoon's confrontation. She could still see the murderous look in his dark eyes as she proclaimed her love for him. Elise sighed again.

"Elise? Is that you?" Her father called from inside the room.

Elise wiped the tears from her face and took a deep breath before pushing open the door.

As it had every day since she arrived, Elise's heart swelled with pride as she spied her handsome father propped against his pillow. She marveled at how strong he looked, even in the midst of his illness. He actually appeared to be thriving.

She paused in the doorway, wishing she had the courage to throw her arms around him and tell him how much she loved him. Her feet and arms remained frozen in place. It was no use. She was a coward. She would rather return to Boston carrying the fragile hope of one day returning to earn his love, than bear forever the pain and burden of his rejection.

"How was your trip to town this morning? Rosa tells me you and Tanner went into Crossroads to do some shopping."

Elise flinched at the mention of Tanner's name. "It was fine, sir."

Seth didn't miss the unhappiness in her voice. It was just as he feared. She didn't like it. What was he thinking anyway? Did he honestly believe that Crossroads could measure up to Boston?

"I received a letter from Aunt Claudia today."

Seth held his tongue. Rosa warned him about disparaging her aunt in front of Elise. That was no way to endear himself to his daughter.

Elise, however, mistook his lack of response for a lack of interest. Though her heart sagged with disappointment, she tried to sound cheerful as she continued, "both she and Mr.

Bennett are coming to take me home."

The color drained slowly from Seth's face as her words registered in his mind and drove a dagger through his heart. Going home? No! She couldn't go back to Boston. Not now, not yet. She didn't love him yet.

Tanner entered the room before Seth could respond to his daughter. "Seth, I need to talk to you. Alone."

Seth heard the urgency in Tanner's voice and yet the desperation in his own heart refused to give way. His little girl was going to leave. Nothing was more important than that. "Later, Tanner," Seth dismissed him without looking up. "Elise and I are talking right now."

"It won't wait."

Seth's brows raised in astonishment at the grave tone in Tanner's voice. He knew it must be something serious. Reluctantly, he gave in. "Elise, would you excuse us for a moment?"

Elise knew the reason for Tanner's visit. He was reporting her duplicity to her father. She didn't hold it against him. In fact, it made her love him all the more. After all, Tanner was just protecting the one he loved. She would have done the same thing had the situation been reversed.

She left without protest, too ashamed to face her father. She couldn't bear to see his face when he heard what she had done.

Tanner stood silently before Seth, shifting his weight uncomfortably as he searched for the right words to say. His heart ached so badly right now, he could hardly think. He knew what he had to do, but it hurt so much. How could he repeat vile things about the woman he loved? He felt like a traitor.

But what about Seth? Tanner owed him his life. The

decision was made. No matter the cost, Tanner had to protect him.

"Well?" Seth prodded. "What is it?"

"Sir, it's about your daughter." Tanner hesitated for a moment. "What I've got to say isn't pretty, sir. I just want you to know I wouldn't say it if there were any other way."

"Say what, Tanner?" Seth snapped impatiently. "I've never known you to mince words. Tell me what it is you've got to say."

"She's deceived you, sir."

"Deceived me?" Seth repeated for clarification. "Deceived me?"

The words cut deeply through Tanner as he spoke them. "Seth, doesn't it seem a bit odd that you've heard nothing from her all these years and she suddenly shows up at your door when she hears you're dying?"

Seth narrowed his gaze. "What are you getting at?"

"That the reason she's here is not concern for your health." He swallowed hard before continuing, "That she's only here for your money."

Tanner braced himself for an explosive response, but Seth said nothing. He simply stared.

"I'm sorry, Seth. You'll never know how sorry." Tanner dragged his long fingers through his dark hair. "I know it's hard to believe, I can hardly believe it myself, but I talked to her. I confronted her with my suspicions and she didn't deny them. She's fooled us both, sir." Tanner shoved his hands into his pockets and stared at the polished floor. "You've always been like a father to me. I just can't stand by and watch you get hurt."

"Then don't."

Tanner thought at first he imagined the voice. No one, upon hearing of such cruel betrayal, could respond so coolly. He looked up and his eyes locked with the emerald green ones of his employer. He'd never seen the look of raw determination that now glittered in his eyes.

"Seth?"

"I mean it." Seth's voice was emotionless. "Go on. We've got plenty of business to tie up over in Fort Worth. You can ride out tomorrow morning. By the time you finish the cattle negotiations and get back, she'll be gone."

Tanner was completely astonished by his cool demeanor. "Seth, did you understand what I said? Elise is only after your money."

"I understand perfectly. You ride out at first light."

Tanner shook his head in protest. "I'm sorry, sir, I can't do that. You might need—"

"I don't need anything!" Seth pounded his fists into the mattress as he shouted, "I especially don't need you, so get out!"

Elise had returned to wait outside her father's door in hopes that after Tanner finished, she would muster the courage to explain everything. She arrived just in time to hear her father throw Tanner out, to reject the man he loved as a son.

Hot tears bathed her face as she ran blindly to her room. She pulled the door closed and slumped wearily against it. To know that she'd failed to win her father's love was painful, but to think she'd driven a wedge between the two men she loved was unbearable.

thirteen

Unmindful of the turmoil that rocked the Garver ranch, the morning dawned brightly, ushering in a beautiful new day. Yet even the sight of bright golden sunlight, streaming through her bedroom window, failed to dislodge the heaviness of Elise's heart.

She lay motionless under the blankets, staring up at the ceiling. She had never known such despair in her life. It finally happened. Her seemingly endless reserve of optimism had dried up.

She needed to get away, to think things out someplace away from distraction. That shouldn't be too difficult. After all, Texas was a pretty big state. She sat up with new determination, and swung her feet over the side of the bed.

She dressed quickly, slipping into the pumpkin orange, calico riding skirt hanging from a hook in the wardrobe. The lavender blouse she donned was chosen solely because it hung closest to the front of the cabinet. She was too depressed to care whether it matched or not.

She bent to select a bonnet for her ride, when the black felt hat that Tanner had chosen for her caught her eye. She picked it up, gently caressing the brim. If she closed her eyes tightly she could remember the look on Tanner's face when he had placed it on her head. For that brief moment, he had loved her, she had seen it in his dark eyes. She hugged the hat to her chest. She would wear it today.

Elise decided not to take the time to pile her mass of dark hair on top of her head in its usual elaborate coiffure, opting instead to wear it in one long braid as she had seen Rosa do. She knew it wasn't a proper hairstyle, Mrs. Rhoades would certainly not approve, but for once, Elise didn't care. Who would see her, anyway?

She finished tying off the braid as she stepped off the bottom stair. The empty place in the hall where Becky usually reclined indicated her master wasn't present. Elise slipped into the kitchen. "Has he left already?"

"Who?"

"Tanner. Has Tanner gone?" Her voice was tinged with despair.

"Sure, honey, he left at first light. Says he's got business in Fort Worth he needs to clear up." Rosa's smile faded at the sight of Elise's downcast face. "Is there a problem, *querida*?"

Elise's shoulders slumped in disappointment. "No, I only hoped I could see him before he left." She started to turn back toward the door.

"Don't worry, honey, he's never gone more than a couple of days. He'll be back in no time."

"No time will be too late," Elise whispered as she stepped into the hall.

"Wait, where are you going?" Rosa bustled after her, wringing her hands. "You can't go yet. You haven't had any breakfast."

"I'm not hungry. I thought I'd do a little riding this morning."

"What is it? Is there a problem? Can I fix it?"

Elise's lips curved upward as she shook her head. "No,

I'm afraid not. I've got to handle this one alone."

Rosa placed a comforting hand on her shoulder. "Never alone, *querida*. Remember, you are a Christian now. You are never alone."

"I guess I'd forgotten." She opened the back door and stepped outside. "Don't hold lunch for me. I won't be back till later."

Rosa watched from the doorway as Elise made her way across the yard and disappeared into the stables. *It looks bad, Father*, she prayed with a shake of her head. *Poor girl's hurting. I don't know what the problem is, but I'm thankful You do. Help her, Lord. Help her to see You. Amen.*

Elise found James working in the stables and he was more than happy to saddle Miss Sadie for her. In a matter of minutes, she was directing the mare out into the bright sunlight.

She bent over to whisper in Miss Sadie's ear. "I need some time alone. How about you?"

Miss Sadie seemed to sense her rider's mood and, with a burst of speed, the twosome was galloping across the yard toward the wide-open range.

⁊ፆ

Rosa swung the heavy wooden panel open with a crash. "Okay, *Señor* Garver," she demanded, "just what is going on around here?"

"Rosa!" Seth shouted, "You 'bout scared me out of my wits."

"Then it couldn't have been much of a scare," Rosa quipped. She could see the beginning of a protest on Seth's lips and she raised a hand to silence him. "What's going on with Elise and Tanner?"

Seth folded his arms across his chest and looked out the

window, refusing to meet her penetrating stare. "I don't know what you mean."

"You most certainly do," she accused. She strode over to stand beside his bed. "Why did Tanner ride out of here this morning looking like he'd lost his best friend, and why is Elise so upset she won't eat?"

Seth shrugged noncommittally. "Maybe a little tiff?"

"Seth, I am at the end of my patience with you. I've stood back, watching you play the invalid, hoping you knew what you were doing. I can see now that you've made a complete mess of things, and I need to step in and fix them up."

He looked at her then, his eyes filled with pain. "It's too late, Rosa. She's going home."

Rosa dropped into the chair beside his bed. "Elise is going home?" she repeated for confirmation. "To Boston?"

Seth nodded. "She got a letter from Claudia. The old crab is on her way to Texas right now. With that Bennett fella."

"Bennett fella? Where have I heard that name?" Rosa racked her memory for his identity. "Oh, no, the man Claudia mentioned in her letter. What a mess!" she exclaimed as the full import of Seth's words sunk in. "I forgot all about Elise being engaged. No wonder Tanner looked so bad."

"That's only part of it. Tanner's upset with me, too. I practically threw him out."

Rosa's dark eyes flashed angrily. "You did what?"

"I had to, Rosa. He knows why Elise is here. He was going to protect me from her." Seth laughed bitterly at the irony of his words. "I couldn't let him come between us. I had to send him away. There's so little time left."

"Slow down, Seth, you lost me somewhere. Why would Tanner think you need to be protected from Elise?"

"He's talked to her. I'm not sure how it came up, but he asked her why she came to see me, and she told him it was for my money."

Rosa gasped. "That can't be true. Elise isn't like that. Besides, she already has your money. Claudia's been living on your money for years. Elise too. Why would she have to come here?"

"I don't know." Seth shrugged his broad shoulders. "Maybe Claudia was afraid I didn't have everything written out, you know, to make it legal that they get everything when I die."

"The very idea of it makes me sick. I just can't believe it of Elise."

"Don't hold it against her. After all, think of who raised her. As greedy as old Claudia is, it's no wonder she's trained Elise to think the same way. The way I figure it, it's my own fault for giving the child away."

Rosa's mind was reeling. Elise had told Tanner she was only here for her father's money? Something was not right. "Look, Seth, I don't know what's going on, but the Lord does. Let's take this to Him."

To her surprise, Seth didn't argue. "That's a good idea, Rosa. Let's pray."

❧

Horse and rider appeared as one as they sailed effortlessly across the grassy fields. Elise leaned into the horse, rolling comfortably with the now-familiar gait. Riding never failed to exhilarate her and this morning was no exception. The breeze and sunlight had a healing effect on her aching heart.

Upon sighting the circle of trees marking the pond on the horizon, Elise slowed Miss Sadie. "There it is, girl." She pointed straight ahead. "There's the spot we're looking for."

Again, she picked up the pace, not stopping until they reached the cool shade of the spreading oaks. Elise slid out of the saddle and secured Miss Sadie's reins around a low-hanging branch of a tree. "You rest here. I'll be back later," she promised, patting the horse's velvety nose.

The sight of the pond brought a rush of memories flooding back to Elise. It seemed like ages ago that she and Rosa had spent a carefree afternoon here. Her life was so full of promise then. What a difference a few days could make.

She gave her head a shake, dismissing the melancholy thought. No point in reliving the past. Better to concentrate on the future.

Without Rosa to coax her, Elise felt no draw to the crystalline water. Instead, she crawled up on the wall of rocks, settled back against a sun-warmed boulder, and closed her eyes.

Myriad thoughts vied for her attention. Was it wrong to come to Texas? Was it pure selfishness to want her father's love? If only she'd been satisfied with what she had, none of this mess would have happened. If she hadn't come to Texas, there would be no rift between the two men she loved.

If she had been content to settle for dreams, she wouldn't have this heartbreak now of never hearing her father tell her he loved her.

Yet, no dream was as sweet as seeing him, really seeing him, had been. And perhaps the pleasure of talking with him face to face was worth the price of not hearing the words she needed so badly to hear.

If she'd stayed in Boston, she'd probably be married by now. She'd never have met tall, handsome Tanner nor felt the pain of his rejection.

But perhaps the joy of being in love, the giddy head-over-heels feeling she'd known when he kissed her was worth the pain she was suffering. After all, she might never feel that alive again.

She didn't know Mr. Bennett very well; they'd met only once or twice before, but she knew it would be a marriage of convenience. She doubted she would ever have the strong feelings for him that she had for Tanner.

So what should she do? Should she take the memories she'd gathered back with her to Boston to live and relive for the rest of her life, and leave Tanner and her father to their lives? Or should she take what little time she had left and press for their love, possibly at the cost of their relationship?

Elise sighed heavily. She felt so very alone.

Suddenly, Rosa's words came back to her. "Not alone. You're a Christian now. Never alone."

Elise bowed her head. "Oh, God, I know it's awfully late to ask You, but what do I do now?"

❧

The sun had begun its slow descent when Elise galloped up to the stables. James met her at the door. "Good, you're back! You've got company up at the house. I was gonna ride out looking for you."

"Company?" Elise squealed with delight. Could it be? She kicked the horse up and raced around to the front door. Her face fell at the sight that greeted her.

Aunt Claudia stood grim-faced on the porch with Mr. Bennett close at her side.

"There she is now!" Rosa called, pointing out Elise as she rounded the corner.

"Look at you!" Claudia's steely gray eyes nearly bulged from their sockets.

Astonished and pleased that Aunt Claudia was impressed by something she'd done, Elise smiled as she patted the horse's neck. "Oh yes, ma'am, I ride all the time. Are you surprised?"

Claudia dismissed her with a curt wave of her hand. "Don't be such a simpleton. I'm not talking about your riding. Look at your clothes! That color combination is horrible, even for your pitiful standards." She looked to her companion. "She's a trial, Percival. Positively hopeless."

Percival snickered.

"Elise is a fine rider," Rosa pointed out in her defense. "She shows a lot of promise."

"I don't recall asking for your opinion. And I can't believe that you've already finished with our unpacking. Get busy." She turned her imperious glare toward Elise. "Elise, is it too much to ask for you to get down off that beast and join us?" she barked impatiently. "Mr. Bennett and I have come an awfully long way to see you. How rude of you to keep us waiting."

Elise kept her gaze downcast. "Yes ma'am, I'll be right there." Slowly she reined Miss Sadie around and headed to the stables.

"Did you see your people?" James asked eagerly. "Bet

they were proud to see what a fine horsewoman you've become."

Elise shrugged. "I don't think so, James."

He did not miss the disappointment in her voice. "Aw, Miss Garver. They just don't know any better, being city folks and all."

"Thank you," Elise said with a half-hearted smile. "Would you take care of Miss Sadie for me? I need to hurry back up to the house."

"Sure will. And did I mention how purty you're looking? Just like a flower."

She brightened momentarily, flashing him a grateful smile. "I'm glad you think so. Good night."

⁂

Elise closed the back door behind her without a sound and tiptoed down the hall, hoping to get up to her room undetected. No such luck. Aunt Claudia met her at the top of the stairs.

"Elise, did you or did you not bring your copy of *Mrs. Rhoades's Complete handbook of Courteous Behavior and Social Graces For Young Women* with you like I told you to?"

"Yes ma'am, I did."

"And did you consult the book before you selected that . . .that ensemble?" she demanded disdainfully.

"No ma'am. I did not."

"Of course not!" she snapped. "I am certain Mrs. Rhoades would never advocate a young woman going out so poorly attired. Your hair and clothes are a disgrace. What will Mr. Bennett think? And that hat." Claudia's arm snaked out as if to grab it, and Elise backed up quickly, pulling the hat from her head and wrapping her arms around it. Claudia was seething. "Well? What do you have to say for yourself?"

"I'm quite thankful Mrs. Rhoades isn't here to see me."

Aunt Claudia was not amused. She fixed Elise with a condemning glare. "Bad blood will always tell."

Elise was familiar with the accusation. She heard it all the time. She learned it was best to say nothing in her own defense. "I'm certain you are correct, Aunt Claudia. Now, if you will excuse me, I need to change before I see Mr. Bennett."

"Mr. Bennett and I are exhausted from our travel. He told me to tell you he has retired for the evening. Since you haven't a civil tongue in your head, I will retire as well." With that, she turned and stalked down the hall in a huff.

ta

It was late when with a sigh of resignation, Elise crawled between the crisp white sheets. She would not cry or complain. After all, it was in God's hands now.

This afternoon, when she'd prayed, she finally decided to cast all her cares upon Him. She would trust God for her future. She hadn't received immediate direction. The clouds did not part as she breathed her "Amen," no words appeared on the glossy surface of the water telling her what to do, yet she knew she could trust Him. She would let Him lead.

When James had met her with the news of her company, her heart skipped a beat. She'd thought that God's answer was Tanner, that somehow, miraculously, he'd come home.

When instead she saw her aunt's disapproving scowl, she took that to be God's answer. She belonged in Boston. Her memories would have to be enough.

Tanner smoothed out the corner of his bedroll, then lay back with his arms folded behind his head to stare up into the starlit sky. There was little breeze tonight, nothing to disturb the silence that settled comfortably over the land.

Becky nuzzled up beside him. "Made good time today, Becky. We'd be halfway to Fort Worth by now if I hadn't . . ." he paused, "Just what would you call what I did? Reconsidered? Saw the light? Changed my mind or just lost it?" Tanner chuckled at his little joke. "Guess there's a little truth in all those things."

This morning there had been no softening of his resolve. He rode out at first light, just as Seth had commanded. That hurt, no doubt about it. He loved Seth like a father and it was painful to feel the sting of his rejection. He'd wanted to protect him, and was thrown out for his efforts.

Fact was, he had tried to tell himself it suited him just fine, he didn't want to be around that Garver woman, anyway. She'd shown her true colors. Despite the fact she looked and smelled like an angel, she was a gold digger, pure and simple. How could he have been such a fool to fall in love with her? The bitterness of her betrayal had fueled his ride most of the morning.

But, without warning, sometime during the course of the day, a doubt had taken seed in his mind. Was it really that simple?

As he made his trek east, he had continued to replay all the events. He could remember clearly the bright blush on her creamy white cheeks when he'd confronted her with his accusations. That was proof, wasn't it?

Perhaps, but a blush was hardly conclusive evidence.

After all, didn't those same smooth cheeks flame with the slightest provocation?

She had wanted to explain herself. Tanner had tried to erase from his memory the pleading look in her green eyes as she tried to offer an explanation. He had refused. He was hurting so badly, he didn't want to hear anymore. Now, from somewhere deep within himself the realization emerged—you should have heard her out.

She lied to me—she doesn't love me—she's engaged, he had argued. *But,* came the rebuttal, *you love her anyway.*

It was a little past four in the afternoon when Tanner had stopped. He'd bowed his head and prayed. "Lord God, I don't know what to do. Seems like I'm slow to learn to bring things to You in prayer, but I'm here now. I only hope it's not too late. Please show me what to do."

Tanner grinned at the memory. There he'd sat, stock-still, in the middle of a deserted road, waiting to hear from God. The amazing thing was, he did!

Not audibly, of course, but the leading was so clear, he didn't hesitate. Without a second's delay, he had reined Gypsy around and galloped toward home. He'd trust God to know what to do when he got there.

Tanner shifted, pulling the blanket up under his chin for protection against the cool night air. "I don't know, Becky. I'd be lying if I said I wasn't mixed up. But this much I know. I love her. And I've got to go home."

fourteen

Elise rose early and slipped quietly down the stairs and into the kitchen.

"Good morning, Rosa."

Rosa met her at the door and enveloped Elise in her arms. She didn't know what was going on, but she knew she loved Elise—that was enough. She'd trust God to take care of the details. "Good morning, *querida*." She held Elise at arm's length, her dark eyes studying the younger woman's face. "Did you sleep well? I was afraid you'd be starving, so I fixed a big breakfast for you. Don't tell Rosa you're not hungry; it would break my heart."

Elise laughed. "I'm famished."

"*Bueno,* good." Rosa walked to the stove and returned to the table, carrying a full plate. She motioned for Elise to sit down. "You eat every bite."

Elise slid into the chair. "You are too good to me, Rosa."

"Nonsense. You and I are part of the same family, God's family, and I always take care of my family."

Elise bit into a fluffy biscuit and chewed thoughtfully. "What did you think about my other family? Aunt Claudia and Mr. Bennett, I mean."

Rosa took a long draught of her coffee to give herself time to fashion an acceptable answer. "Your aunt is exactly as I expected," she said with a forced smile, "and Mr. Bennett, well, he's uh, he's. . .here!" Rosa was on her feet instantly.

140

Elise turned to look up at the man standing behind her. "Good morning, Mr. Bennett. I am surprised to see you up so early."

"Couldn't sleep," he grumbled. "Too quiet here. Don't know how you've been able to stand it so long." He took the seat Rosa vacated and studied Elise's breakfast with interest. "Get me a plate, too," he instructed Rosa.

Bennett lowered his voice only slightly as he leaned over to confide in Elise, "This country cooking is terrible. I can hardly get it past my lips. Of course, a man's got to keep up his strength." He patted the elaborate brocade vest covering his stomach. "At least it's filling."

Her emerald eyes flashed indignantly as she enunciated, "Rosa is an excellent cook, Mr. Bennett. And a dear friend. Please be careful how you address her."

Bennett was momentarily stunned into silence. "Never known you to contradict me, Elise." He wagged a finger at her. "It's most unladylike of you. And frankly, the idea of you, fraternizing with the domestic help is scandalous. I can see there are many things we will have to work on once we are married."

Rosa stomped over to the table and slapped a plate in front of him. Sensing an impending storm, Elise sent her a beseeching look, and Rosa reluctantly turned away without comment.

Bennett didn't seem to notice anything amiss as he dug into his breakfast with gusto. "After breakfast, I'd like to see the place. Quite a ranch here. Very profitable, I'd say."

"Are you interested in ranching, Mr. Bennett?" Elise found her appetite was gone, so she busied herself moving the food around the plate.

"Not particularly, but I'm very interested in seeing what

I bargained for."

Elise lowered her fork to her plate and looked over to give him her full attention. "I'm not certain I know what you mean, Mr. Bennett."

"Just as well." He dismissed the topic with a wave of his fork before stuffing a huge bite of steak into his mouth. "Anyway," he managed between bites, "after breakfast we'll mount up and tour the place."

"Do you ride?"

"Yes, my dear. I know it's difficult to believe a man of my refinement would take an interest in equestrian diversion but, in truth, I've spent many a pleasant hour astride a fine thoroughbred."

Elise found her first genuine smile since Mr. Bennett had joined her at the table. He liked to ride. She knew it would be important for them as husband and wife to share some common interest, and until now she was unaware of any similarities between them. This was great. They could share a love of riding. She smiled broadly. God *had* been listening to her prayers.

"If you'll excuse me, Mr. Bennett, I'd like to go change for our ride."

"Good enough," he said with a nod, cramming an entire biscuit into his mouth. "I'll meet you at the stables in one hour. And be prompt, Elise. Remember, a Bennett is always punctual."

Rosa followed Elise out into the hall with a bundle in her arms. "Wait, *querida*. Take this for your ride. I made it for you."

Elise accepted it with a protest. "But I have the skirts of your daughter's."

"*Sí*, that is true," Rosa nodded, "But I want you to have

one of your very own." Tears glittered in her dark eyes and her voice broke as she whispered, "Maybe you'll think of me when you wear it."

Elise's eyes widened with understanding. The riding outfit was a farewell gift from Rosa. Elise threw her arms around the older woman and hugged her tightly. "Oh Rosa, I don't know if I can bear it. I'll miss you so." Tears rolled down her cheeks. "You're my dearest friend, and I'll never ever forget you."

Rosa backed away, brushing the tears from her eyes. "Get upstairs now. Remember," she teased, "a Bennett is always punctual."

Elise climbed the stairs slowly, her troubles momentarily forgotten as she studied the garment, her brow furrowed. From behind her Rosa called quietly, "It's navy. Any color blouse would match nicely."

"How did you know what I...?" Elise turned around and smiled sheepishly. "Thanks, Rosa. Thank you for everything."

After a quick change, Elise hurried to the stables. "Good morning, James. Would you saddle Miss Sadie for me please? And Mr. Bennett will need a mount as well."

James turned around and his mouth gaped open at the sight. "Miss Garver, is it you?"

She felt the blush burn all the way to her feet. She nodded shyly.

"Why yer, yer," he struggled to find the right word, "elegant! That's it. Yer elegant. Like one of them ladies in the magazines. Boy howdy, I wish Tanner was here to see you right now."

A wistful sigh escaped as Elise nodded again. "Me, too."

"If you'll notice, Mr. Bennett, that's the bunkhouse up ahead," Elise extended her gloved hand to indicate the structure, "which means we've come full circle. That's the end of our tour. What did you think?"

Silence. "Mr. Bennett?" Upon getting no response, she turned around in her saddle to see what he was up to. She had to bite her tongue to keep from laughing out loud at the sight that met her eyes.

Percival Bennett's horse trailed Miss Sadie by a good five yards, with her disheveled rider clinging to the saddle horn for dear life. To say he sat atop the horse would be overly optimistic, for in truth the man listed so heavily to one side, Elise was uncertain what it was that kept him in his saddle.

"Oh, Mr. Bennett!" she cried, quickly riding to his aid. "Are you all right?"

The glazed look in his blue eyes evaporated at the sound of her voice. "Of course, I'm all right," he snapped indignantly. "Just resting, that's all."

Elise couldn't resist goading him a bit. "How sensible of you. Are you ready to ride out to see the cattle? My father's herd is very impressive."

"No!" he answered quickly, then amended, "What I mean is, uh, this horse is winded. That's it. The horse is winded. Wouldn't be right to take the old nag out again. Most humane thing would be to take her back to the stall."

"Oh, no, Mr. Bennett, Baby is not a nag. She's one of my father's prize mares." She turned her sweetest smile on him. "And don't you worry; I'm certain she'd enjoy the ride out to the far pasture."

"Are you contradicting me, Elise?" Bennett was incredulous. "Highly improper for a woman aspiring to be a

Bennett. I expected better of you."

Elise's cheeks burned brightly with shame. He was right. She'd been deliberately perverse with him. For what purpose? Did she want him to withdraw his offer of marriage? No, indeed. Aunt Claudia would be livid. How many times had she reminded Elise of her duty to marry well. "Mr. Bennett is the epitome of all that is desirable in a man, Elise," she would say, "and you are fortunate that he would even consider you."

She knew Aunt Claudia was right, and yet, she didn't feel too fortunate right now. He might be the height of desirability, but her tastes lately seemed to run a bit more rugged. Someone tall and dark perhaps. . . .

Nonsense, she upbraided herself for her wayward thoughts, *you've prayed about it. It's in God's hands. And if God thinks Mr. Bennett is right, then so be it.*

"I'm sorry, Mr. Bennett. How thoughtless of me."

"Never mind the apology, my dear," his tone softened slightly, "you're obviously overwrought. I have that effect on women." He smiled magnanimously. "It's forgotten. Let's press on to the stables, shall we?"

❧

"You two finished already?" James asked as they walked up to the stable.

"Yes, we are," Bennett said as he slid unceremoniously from his saddle and hit the ground with a dull thud. He pulled a small mirror from the pocket of his coat and studied himself. "My but hair's a fright. Young man?"

James finished lifting Elise from the saddle and placed her gently on the ground before responding, "Sir?"

"You need to go into town for me. I'm out of my pomade for my hair, and this awful Texas wind has ruined me.

I must have a jar right away."

James shook his head. "Sorry, sir, can't do that. Short-handed around here today. I'll be glad to run in for you first thing tomorrow morning."

"Tomorrow? Tomorrow?" Bennett repeated imperiously. "Do you know who you are addressing? Percival Bennett, of the Boston Bennetts. If you value your job, you'll head for town right away."

"Look, Mr. Bennett," James gritted out between his teeth, "work here is priority one. . .not baby-sitting city folks."

"Why you impertinent. . . !" Bennett's face mottled with rage.

Elise slipped between the men and raised her hands for silence. "Please gentlemen. May I make a suggestion? I need to run into town for some ribbon, and I would be happy to purchase Mr. Bennett's hair tonic while I'm there."

"No fiancée of mine will be traipsing around the country unescorted. Think of the disgrace!"

"Then you'll have to make the trip," James said, glaring his challenge, 'cuz I can't spare anyone else today."

The tension between the men in the stables was thick enough to cut with a knife, and it wasn't until after James harnessed the horses to the wagon and Elise was, at last, heading the team toward town, that she could release the breath she had been holding.

She stole a sidelong glance at her companion on the bench who was mumbling under his breath about the inconvenience of the trip. An alarming thought gripped her. *As soon as we get back to Boston, this man is going to be my husband.* She tried to ignore the hollow feeling in the pit of her stomach.

Try to look on the bright side, she told herself. Marriage, even to Mr. Bennett would provide her with the family she so desperately wanted. It wouldn't be the same as her father's love, she knew, but she'd be a Bennett. She'd have someplace to belong and maybe even children to love.

And, she continued to encourage herself, it would be nice to be out from under Aunt Claudia's critical eye. She chewed the corner of her lip. Of course, she wasn't too certain she wouldn't be jumping out of the frying pan and into the fire. Mother Bennett, a rather dour matron and a pinnacle of propriety would be sharing a home with Elise and her husband.

She closed her eyes for a second, shutting out the fearful thought. She tried to replace it with something positive by imagining married life. She could picture herself strolling hand in hand with her husband, with several children scampering around them. She imagined herself saying something to her husband that pleased him and he bent to favor her with a loving smile. His ebony eyes met hers. . . .

Elise started, accidentally jerking the reins. Mr. Bennett stared at her with wide eyes. "What is it, Elise? Trouble with the wagon?"

"Oh, no, everything is fine." She gave an embarrassed shrug. "I'm afraid I was just daydreaming."

"A Bennett is always alert, Miss Garver," he scolded. "Please remember that."

"Yes, Mr. Bennett, I'll try."

Satisfied that she would be more careful, Bennett slumped back against the bench to continue his grumbling, leaving

Elise to consider her daydreams. Mr. Bennett's eyes were a peculiar shade of pale blue, not ebony like the man in her imagination. Those were Tanner's dark orbs infiltrating her dreams.

Forget him, she told herself. *He hates you.* I can't, she argued back. *I love him.*

❧

Tanner galloped to the door of the stables just as James stepped out into the sunlight. "Hey, Tanner! What're you doing home? Thought you were in Fort Worth."

"Change of plans. You seen Elise?"

James nodded. "Yep. She and some city fella rode into town. Left here about ten minutes ago."

"Thanks." Tanner pushed his dark hat lower on his brow and kicked up his horse, galloping off in a cloud of dust. He and Gypsy made good time by cutting across a field, and they closed in undetected on the wagon in a matter of minutes. From his vantage point, he could see Elise at the reins and a man beside her on the bench.

Tanner swallowed hard. In spite of his confidence that he was doing exactly what God wanted him to do, he suddenly felt nervous. As he galloped up to the wagon, he steeled himself for his meeting with the competition.

He reined the horse up on Elise's left side. "Morning, Miss Garver," he said, tipping his hat casually as if his appearance were an everyday thing.

"Tanner?" Elise squeaked, nearly dropping the reins. She had to blink twice to make certain the smiling man riding beside her was not a figment of her imagination. "What are you doing here?"

"Had to make a trip into town for supplies." He surveyed the wagon. "Seems you're doing the same thing," he added innocently. "Maybe we can travel together."

"Well, uh. . . ." She glanced nervously toward Mr. Bennett. "I uh. . . ."

Tanner's gaze followed hers. "Hello." He nodded politely to the man beside her before turning back to Elise. "I thought you'd be with your fiancé. Isn't he here?"

Elise blushed. "This *is* my fiancé. This is Mr. Percival Bennett."

Tanner was stunned. He hoped the shock he felt didn't register on his face. This was the competition? He turned toward the man again. "Well, hello there!" His warm greeting dripped with hospitality. "We've heard so much about you; it's a pleasure finally to meet you." He silently congratulated himself on his quick recovery.

This was Elise's fiancé? Somehow he'd pictured him differently. Someone tall and sophisticated, someone whose good looks would complement hers. Not a man old enough to be her father, who was balding and overweight to boot.

It's not what you think. Isn't that what she said? What an understatement. Tanner shoved his dark hat down on his head. It was time to find out what was going on. He urged Gypsy around to the other side of the wagon to get some answers. "So," he said, striking up a conversation, "the name's Bennett?"

Bennett nodded regally from his perch on the bench. "That's right. Percival Bennett here, of the Boston Bennetts." He looked down the end of his nose to inquire, "And you are?"

"Tanner Dalton, one of Seth Garver's hands." He deftly turned the attention back to the other man. "Boston Bennetts, huh? Seems I've heard of the family. . . ," he said.

"I should say you have, sir." He puffed out his chest with pride. "The Bennett family has been a bastion of social refinement and propriety for generations. We trace our lineage all the way back to the royal families of Europe," he boasted. "We have wealth, prestige, and what's more, the rare distinction of an untainted name. Never once in our proud history has even a breath of scandal touched the Bennett name."

Tanner gave a low whistle of appreciation. "That's mighty impressive." Inwardly, he cringed. Had Bennett just given him the evidence to convict Elise as a gold digger? What else besides money could she possibly see in the aged, overbearing windbag?

No. This time he would not jump to conclusions. Elise deserved better than that.

He inclined his head in her direction and lowered his voice. "No slight intended against Miss Garver there, but how is it a child like that ended up with a powerful man of the world like yourself? She must be one lucky woman."

Tanner could tell by the pleased look on the man's face that his strategy had worked. The size of the man's ego was exceeded only by the size of his waistline.

"You're very perceptive for a cowboy, Mr. Dalton. Actually, Miss Garver had nothing to do with it. She's too young and inexperienced to understand these things. The fact is, Claudia Stephens was instrumental in our alliance."

"That must be Miss Garver's Aunt Claudia?"

Bennett nodded. "Shrewd woman. I've handled a few investments for her over the years, always mutually profitable, so when she came to me with a proposition about her niece, I was all ears."

Bennett leaned out from the wagon toward Tanner to confide, "Claudia was concerned about the girl's prospects for marriage. One can never be too careful about that sort of thing. I was willing to overlook her obviously inferior bloodlines," he cast a glance toward Elise, whose attention was directed straight ahead, "because she's a lovely thing, and quite innocent. With the proper training at the hand of my mother, she'll make a fine Bennett."

The party rounded the corner into the town proper just then, and Tanner decided not to press the conversation further. They rode up to the general store in silence. After helping Elise and Bennett alight from the wagon, he lingered outside for a moment to tend the horses and sort things out.

Bennett spoke of his engagement to Elise as unemotionally as one would describe any business venture. He never once mentioned love or mutual respect or any of the ingredients Tanner would have assumed would go into a marriage proposal. Tanner felt sick. Poor Elise. How could he have ever have been so wrong? And what could he do now to make it right?

As he stood by the team in front of the store window, he prayed. "God, show me what You want me to do. Amen."

Tanner stepped inside the store and paused to locate Elise. He started toward the back of the room where she was standing with Bennett, when he heard muttering coming from behind the counter. He leaned over to see Nathan, down on all fours. "Problem?"

"Huh?" Nathan glanced up in surprise. "Oh, howdy, Tanner. Didn't hear you come in. I spilled these nails and just wasted a good-half hour picking 'em up. Don't know why they can't build a better box to keep them in." He dusted off his pants as he got to his feet. "Kinda surprised to see you in here again so soon." Nathan leaned across the counter with a twinkle in his eye. "How's the pretty little woman."

Tanner failed to make the connection. "Little woman?"

"You know," Nathan winked knowingly, "the one you were kissing in my store."

Tanner glanced toward Bennett and Elise. Luckily, they did not seem to hear. "She's fine, thanks." He hoped his unenthusiastic response would quell Nathan's curiosity.

"Oh, I get it," Nathan persisted. "Don't want to talk about her, being she's the boss's daughter and all." He winked again. "Funny, I never figured you for the shy type."

From the corner of his eye, Tanner could see Bennett and Elise making their way toward the counter, and he knew the time for subtlety had passed. If Bennett heard Nathan's prattle, Elise's engagement would be ruined. Kissing one of the ranch hands would be just the sort of situation the Bennett clan liked to avoid.

Suddenly, Tanner smiled.

"Well, Miss Garver!" Nathan exclaimed, glancing nervously between her and Tanner. "Didn't know you were here." He shrugged apologetically at Tanner, before turning back to her. "What can I do for you, ma'am?"

"Nothing for me, thanks, but Mr. Bennett here needs your assistance with some hair preparations."

Nathan stepped out from behind the counter. "Yes, sir. I'll be glad to show you what I've got. Right this way."

Tanner caught Elise's arm before she could follow them. "Wait. I need to ask you something." He felt his heart melt as she raised emerald eyes to meet his. "Is this what you want? Marriage to Bennett?"

She didn't answer immediately. Instead, she dropped her gaze to her hands. A long moment passed before she looked at him again. This time, tears glittered in her eyes. "No," she said simply.

Tanner breathed a loud sigh of relief. He reached out to stroke her silken cheek. "I know I've been a fool, I don't deserve anything from you, but do you think you could find it in your heart to forgive me?"

A large tear slid from her eye as she nodded.

He took her chin and gently tipped her face up to his. "I love you, Elise. I won't lose you."

She smiled tremulously in response as more tears fell.

"Why the tears?" he asked softly.

"I'm trapped in an engagement to a man I do not love and will love forever a man I cannot have."

Tanner resisted the urge to sweep her into his arms. She loved him. God was so good. He gently brushed the tears away with his finger. "Things could change."

She shook her head sadly. "Not this time. Aunt Claudia and Mr. Bennett have finalized all the arrangements. I have nothing to say about it." Her tone was hopeless. "You don't know them, Tanner. Once they've made a decision, it would take nothing short of a miracle to stop them."

fifteen

"You comfortable enough back there, Bennett?" Tanner called over his shoulder.

"I most certainly am not," Bennett snapped from his seat on the floor of the wagon, directly behind Elise, where he sat with his back against the side plank. "A sack of flour provides pitiful little insulation against the pits in this rotten road. And your dog stinks."

"You have my apologies, sir. A fine gentleman like yourself shouldn't have to accept such crude accommodations. You know you're welcome to ride my horse."

Bennett glanced fearfully at the enormous black beast tied to the back of the wagon. "No, no indeed." His voice became hopeful, "Perhaps I could join you two on the bench?"

Tanner shook his dark head. "Sorry, Bennett, it's strictly a two-seater. If you could handle a team, you and I could trade places. But seeing as how you can't, I'll have to drive. Wouldn't do to have Miss Garver at the reins, not when there are two healthy men around. Just isn't done in these parts. A man like yourself understands the importance of propriety."

"Indeed I do. It's just. . . ," he cast a longing look at the bench. "How much longer to the ranch?"

"Not more than twenty minutes." Tanner smiled reassuringly. "Sit back and enjoy the view."

Bennett's silence lasted only briefly. "Is it always so hot here?" he complained.

Tanner nodded again. "Aw, this is nothing. Come August, it's so hot, it's hard to draw a breath." Bennett could not see the wicked smile hovering around Tanner's mouth as he continued, " 'Course, folks around here got a solution. Why, Miss Garver is already a big proponent of it."

"And what would that be?" Bennett sounded bored.

"Skinny dipping," Tanner pronounced casually, carefully ignoring Elise's gasp of horror and Mr. Bennett's sharp intake of breath. "Isn't that right, Miss Garver? Tell him how nice and cool the pond is."

Elise's flushed expression was pained. "Tanner, I don't think Mr. Bennett is interested. . . ."

"No need to be shy, Miss Garver. Mr. Bennett's a practical man; he understands the need for comfort. Besides, he's your intended." Tanner swung around on the bench to face Bennett. "And let me put any worries you might have to rest. The pond we're talking about is real private. Only me and Rosa were there with your fiancée." He turned back to the team before Bennett could see his smile.

"You were there?" Bennett choked. "With Miss Garver?"

Tanner's head bobbed up and down enthusiastically. "Well sure. Sounds a bit crowded I suppose, but actually, it's a real big pond."

"You and Miss Garver. . . ?" Bennett couldn't seem to make himself finish.

"Isn't it nice to know we've become such close friends?" He flashed a cheerful smile over his shoulder. " 'Course," he added thoughtfully, "I guess we were obliged to get to know each other pretty quick, what with her sleeping in my arms and all."

Elise gasped and gripped the bench to keep from falling from the wagon.

"Guess that sounds pretty compromising, but you'd have to understand the circumstances."

Elise turned hope-filled eyes to Tanner and nodded for him to continue.

"Yes, yes, tell me," Bennett's words came out in a rush, "What were the circumstances?"

Tanner shrugged. "Simple, really. You see, we were so warm and comfortable on that mattress, one of us was bound to fall asleep."

"Mattress?" Bennett's voice was a loud, high-pitched squeak.

Tanner ignored the man's distress. "Look here." He pointed up ahead. "We're back already. Wasn't that a quick trip." He turned to smile into Bennett's beet red face. "Bennett, I wouldn't be surprised if all this riding has made you a bit stiff. You know, Miss Garver here had the same trouble." He patted Elise's shoulder companionably. "We found a bath to be the most soothing. Seemed to melt the aches away."

"*We* found?" Bennett's voice sounded weaker.

Tanner stopped the wagon in front of the house. "That's right. Now, of course, you won't be wanting one of them flowery smelling ones like Miss Garver," he added helpfully. "Though I've got to say, it smelled real fine to me."

"Tanner! I don't think Mr. Bennett wants to hear any more—"

"You're right!" Bennett shouted as he scrambled from the back of the wagon and marched stiff-legged up the stairs of the house. "I've heard all I want to hear."

The sound of the door slamming loosened Elise's tongue. "Tanner Dalton! What would make you tell him all those things?" she demanded incredulously. "He's likely to take them all the wrong way." Her eyes flew open with her next fearful thought and she gasped, "He'll probably even tell Aunt Claudia." Elise wrung her hands. "What do you think will happen now?"

Tanner shoved his black hat back from his forehead and grinned down at her, his dark eyes twinkling. "Nothing short of a miracle."

sixteen

"Claudia?" Bennett shouted as he swept into the house. "Claudia?"

Rosa stepped out from the kitchen. "No need to holler, *Señor*. She is upstairs with *Señor* Garver."

Bennett was too overwrought to consider the impropriety of his actions as he took the stairs two at a time, raced down the hall, and exploded into Seth's room unannounced. "The deal's off!" he pronounced with his last burst of energy before collapsing into a chair, gasping for breath.

"What's the matter with you, Percival?" Claudia demanded from her place at the window. "What are you talking about?"

"I've just ridden halfway across Texas on a plank is what's the matter with me," he answered irritably. "And I'm talking about your niece. She doesn't suit. The deal's off."

Seth's interest was piqued. He sat up in bed, shoving his pillows behind him for support. "What deal?"

"Shut up, Seth!" Claudia snapped at her brother-in-law before whipping her head around to glare at Bennett. "Now look here, Bennett," she snarled, "the deal's been made. There's no backing out."

Bennett shook his balding head with defiance. "The deal was that I marry your niece, a sweet, innocent girl with a malleable disposition. Someone deserving of the Bennett name." He wagged an accusing finger at Claudia. "Your niece is neither malleable nor innocent. And this entire ranch wouldn't be worth the blemish she'd bring to my name."

"What ranch?" Seth became more agitated. "And what deal?"

"Shut up, Seth!" Claudia reddened.

Elise and Tanner arrived outside Seth's door in time to hear Claudia's rebuke. Elise gasped her outrage. How dare Aunt Claudia address her father that way. Tanner pressed a finger to his lips and shook his head, imploring her to be silent. He moved back slightly from the door frame, pulling her with him, so as not to be seen.

Bennett shrugged. "What difference does it make if he knows? He hasn't got long to live." He ignored Claudia's threatening scowl and turned to Seth. "Claudia and I have been business associates for some time. I make investments for her," he said by way of explanation.

"Several months ago," he continued, "Claudia came to me with a proposition. She needed someone to marry her niece. Elise is getting to a marriageable age, and it wouldn't be long before some fella would marry her and carry her off. Without the support you send for Elise, Claudia would be a penniless spinster."

Claudia obviously took offense at his remark and fixed him with a frosty glare.

"That's why she needed me. I could marry Elise and guarantee a comfortable income to Claudia."

"All out of the goodness of your heart, I suppose?" Seth mocked.

Bennett laughed. "Don't be a fool, Garver. I'm a businessman first. This ranch will one day be Elise's, pretty soon from what I can surmise, and if she were married to me, the ranch would be mine. Whether I sold the place or hired someone to run it, there'd be big money involved."

He nodded toward Claudia. "I guaranteed Claudia a percentage. It's unlikely any other suitor would be so generous to Claudia."

Seth suppressed his anger long enough to satisfy his curiosity. "But now you've decided the ranch isn't enough?"

Bennett raised his double chin a notch. "Garver, I'm a man of principle. Your daughter may be wealthy and beautiful, but I've got my good name to consider and hundreds of years of impeccable lineage to protect." He shook his head vehemently. "Elise and her exploits would bring our proud heritage crashing down around us."

"You're a fool, Bennett," Claudia hissed venomously.

"Shut up, Claudia!"

Her mouth fell open in surprise. "How dare you—?"

"How dare *you*?" Seth's eyes flashed with fury. "Try and sell my daughter off for a percentage? To a man old enough to be her father."

Claudia stomped over to Seth's bedside. "She owes it to me," she screeched. "I've raised her, I've put up with her all these years. She owes me."

"Claudia," Seth's voice was suddenly calm, "you've told the lie so long, you've convinced yourself." He shook his head sadly. "You didn't have to put up with her. I wanted her back. I begged you to give my daughter back to me. But you had already turned her against me. She hates me."

Elise wrenched free from Tanner's restraining grip and burst into the room. "Oh, no, Father," she cried as she fell to her knees before him. "I don't hate you. I love you." Tears streamed from her eyes as she confessed, "I've always loved you."

Seth was struck silent. Time stood still as he stared at

Elise, trying to find the truth. She said she loved him. Could it be? He found his answer in her eyes. He extended his arms to her and, as she came to him, he pulled her to his chest and held her tightly. "All these years," he whispered into her hair. "She told me you hated me, that the thought of me gave you nightmares. All these years I thought. . ."

Elise pulled back slightly so she could see his face. Her slender finger traced a tear streak across his whiskered cheek. She shook her head in denial. "I've always loved you. Every day, every hour, every minute. . .always."

Seth looked from his daughter to the woman standing over him. "You. . .you conniving scoundrel. How could you do this?"

"Simple," she said haughtily, without a trace of remorse. "Elise is my meal ticket." She sneered into his astonished face. "It didn't take me long to realize that with her in my possession, my future was guaranteed. You'd do anything for her. No amount of money was too much to send for her. I'd have been a fool to send her back to you."

Bennett spoke up. "Claudia, I'm shocked. Your behavior has been most improper. To provide for oneself is important, but to deprive a father of his daughter?" Bennett shook his head in disapproval. "Shocking."

Claudia turned on him. "Shut up, Percival! How could you possibly understand? You've never been poor. You've never been hungry or cold. Well, I have. My parents had nothing. They died with nothing. I vowed I would never suffer that way again."

"And you shall not," Seth pronounced. "This very day I will establish a trust for you. An income for you for the rest of your life. . .on one condition."

"And that is?"

"That I never see your face again."

"Well!" Claudia huffed.

"I mean it, Claudia. You carry yourself back up to Boston and never come back. Or I promise I'll cut you off without a dime."

"Very decent of you, Garver." Bennett nodded his approval.

Seth turned to him. "And Bennett, I trust I don't have to worry about ever seeing you again?"

"Most assuredly. Texas is no place for a gentleman. I'll be leaving first thing in the morning."

"No, sir." Seth shook his head. "You leave today. Both of you. I'll have James take you back to town as soon as you can get your things packed."

"But—"

"Move!"

⁂

Father and daughter clung to one another long after Bennett and Claudia left the room. Finally, Seth drew back to look at her. "You have to believe me, Elise. I wanted you back. I always wanted you back. I tried everything I knew to do."

"I do believe you." Elise nodded. "Even when you didn't answer my letters, I knew to make it happen."

Seth was incredulous. "Letters? You wrote me letters?"

"Every week."

"I never got one." Seth's voice broke. "I thought you hated me."

"Oh, no," Elise smiled into his troubled eyes, "I love you. I told you so in each letter. I gave them to Aunt Claudia to mail." She shook her head ruefully. "I never dreamed she wasn't sending them to you."

Seth rubbed his chin. "I knew the old girl was evil, but I didn't realize she was capable of anything so low. She must really hate me."

"And yet you agreed to support her?" Elise asked in wide-eyed amazement.

Seth chuckled. "Beats all, doesn't it? I don't know where the idea came from, but you can bet it wasn't mine." He raked a hand through his silver-streaked hair. "The only thing I can figure is that Rosa was praying again. She and God get to running things and I never know what's gonna happen next."

"Oh, I think I do," Elise said with a satisfied smile. "God'll be busy answering the prayers of His children."

seventeen

"I believe I'll have another one of them fine biscuits, Rosa," said Seth, smacking his lips in anticipation.

"That's your fourth one this morning," Rosa scolded. "Your recovery has been quite remarkable, *Señor.*"

Seth scowled good-naturedly. "Guess I deserved that. You gonna tease me about it forever?"

"Tease you, nothing." Tanner wagged his fork at Seth. "I'm far more tempted to skin you alive for scaring me so bad. Here I thought you were dying."

Seth's response was genuinely remorseful. "Tanner, son, I hope you can find it in your heart to forgive me. I know what I did was wrong, but I was desperate."

Elise reached over to pat her father's hand. "Don't fuss at him, Tanner. Under the circumstances, I think he was ingenious." She favored him with a bright smile. "I, for one, am grateful, and I forgive you."

"Don't encourage him, *querida.*" Rosa laughed. "I'd hate to think where he'll go from here."

Seth shook his head. "No worries, Rosa. My days of deceit are over." He beamed at Elise. "I've got my little girl home now."

"Speaking of your little girl," Tanner chimed in. "Mind if I borrow her for a while? Thought maybe she and I might go for a ride."

"That's a fine idea." Seth crammed the biscuit into his mouth and started to stand. "Fine weather for it. Think I'll come, too."

Rosa grabbed his arm and pulled him back into his chair. "No, *Señor*. You can stay here and help me with the dishes."

"But I. . . ."

Rosa cut her eyes meaningfully at him. "I think the young people would like to be alone."

Seth's face fell as he grumbled. "Fine. 'Course, I'll get as fat as ol' Bennett if I don't get some exercise."

Elise and Tanner rose from the table. "Thanks for breakfast, Rosa." Elise slipped her arm through Tanner's, and they started for the door.

"Speaking of Bennett," Seth said, stroking his chin thoughtfully, "there's something I never have understood."

Elise cast a worried look at Tanner before turning to ask, "What's that, Father?"

"Why the man would set up the whole plan with Claudia, even go so far as to travel to Texas to see the ranch, and then back out at the last minute." Seth settled back into his chair and stared up at his daughter. "He said you wouldn't suit." He was truly perplexed as he looked back over the table at Rosa to ask, "What could he possibly find about my little girl that was anything less than perfect. I've never met a more proper lady anywhere."

Tanner winked at Elise whose face was flushed a bright red. "Maybe someday you'll find out, sir."

The two of them ducked into the hall to avoid any more questions and disappeared out the back door in a peal of laughter.

❧

The riders raced into the wind, across the sun-kissed range. Even the horses seemed to sense the joyous spirit of the morning, and Becky cavorted gaily at their sides.

They slowed at the crest of a hill, under a small stand of trees to gaze out across the land. Tanner dismounted, then helped Elise to the ground.

Elise released a deeply contented sigh. "I'll never tire of Texas. There's no more beautiful place on earth."

Tanner wrapped an arm behind her waist and smiled down at her. "Beautiful."

Elise turned her face into the breeze to breathe deeply of the fresh air. "I feel so blessed. God has truly answered my prayers."

"Uh," Tannner began sheepishly, "about prayers. Remember what I said about me handling things pretty well without God?"

Elise nodded. "I remember."

He kicked at the dirt with the toe of his boot. "Well, that was the dumbest thing I've ever said." He focused his dark eyes to meet hers. "I've been thinking about the things you said, you know, about being in God's family and Him caring about us an' all, and I've committed to becoming a man of Bible study and prayer." He took her hand in his. "'Course, I'll be needing your help."

She squeezed his hand and smiled warmly into his face. "It'll be my pleasure."

Becky, who'd disappeared into the underbrush, suddenly appeared at their sides and began to yap excitedly at the twosome.

"What is it, girl?" Elise asked. "Did you find something?"

"Shucks, no." Tanner shook his head in dismay. "She's just a mite impatient. Never could keep a secret." He turned to admonish the dog. "Now, if you'll just mosey on out of here, I'll get on with what I was doing before you interrupted me."

Becky withdrew a respectful distance and sat down with her back to them.

"That's better." Tanner turned back to Elise who was clearly bewildered. "There's something else." He cleared his throat several times and pushed his hat back on his head. "Your father made me a partner—"

"Oh, Tanner," Elise squealed, "I'm so happy for you. It's just as it should be. Father and son running things together."

"Whoa, now. I don't want to be your brother."

She raised startled eyes to his.

"I want to be your husband." He took his hat in his hands. "Will you marry me?"

"Yes!" Elise threw her arms around his neck. "Yes, I'll marry you!"

❧

"Fine ceremony, Reverend Douglas." Seth slapped the younger man on the back. "Appreciate you coming out to officiate."

"Glad to do it, Seth." Reverend Douglas sipped his cup of coffee. "Your little girl's a beauty. I know you're proud to have her back."

Seth beamed. "You bet I am. Have I told you she's here to stay? She and Tanner are gonna settle in the house I built for her mother. 'Course, it's not a very big place. Once there's a couple of young un's around, I figure I'll give them this old barn," he gestured around the room, "and I'll move into their place. I always feel closer to Elizabeth there, anyway."

Rosa appeared at his side. "James says the buggy's ready, *Señor* Garver. Any sign of the newlyweds?"

Seth shook his head. "Not yet. Hope she's not fretting over what colors to wear again."

Rosa nodded. "I'm gonna have to work on her. I'm afraid Claudia's cruel comments about Elise's taste in colors have hurt her. I don't know what it will take to help build her confidence back."

"Rosa! I am disappointed in you," Seth said with a teasing glint in his eyes. "I figured a praying woman like you would have already taken that to God."

"You're right, Seth." Rosa was completely serious. "I'll do it right now." She bowed her head for a brief moment. There was a broad smile on her face when she raised it again. "All done."

The noise in the hall indicated the newlyweds had appeared. Seth and Rosa pressed their way through to the front of the crowd just as Tanner and Elise stepped from the stairs.

Rosa gathered Elise into her arms. "I love you, *querida*."

"I love you, too." Elise kissed her cheek before turning to her father.

"I love you, Father." She hugged him tightly. "And thank you. Thank you for everything."

A heavyset woman pushed her way through the crowd to Elise's side. "Thank heavens I caught you before you left," she puffed, her round face red from exertion.

"Mrs. Teekle!" Elise exclaimed with delight as she took the older woman's hand. "How good to see you. I didn't realize you had made it to the wedding."

"Well sure I did. I was plenty tickled to get your letter invitin' me. Wouldn't have missed it." She rolled her eyes in exasperation. "'Course, I'd have been here on time, if ol' Wilbur wasn't such a slowpoke."

"Wilbur?" Elise inquired politely.

Mavis pointed to a reed-thin man at the edge of the crowd.

"My man. Slower than molasses."

Elise smiled. "I'm so glad you were able to come. May I present my husband, Tanner Dalton. And this is my father, Seth Garver, and my dear friend, Rosa Viegas."

Mavis inclined her head. "Nice to meet all of ya." She wrung her chubby hands. "Actually, honey, there's something I'd like to ask of you, before you go."

"Yes, Mrs. Teekle?"

Mavis seemed hesitant to speak. "It's like this. After I met you on the train, I went home and bragged to a couple of my friends about you. You know, what a fine city lady you were and how you dressed so purty with all them fine colors."

"That's lovely of you to say."

Mavis put up her hand to silence her. "That ain't all. When I told them I was coming to your wedding, and that you were gonna be in Fort Worth, they pestered me half to death asking if you'd come and speak to our women's club."

Mavis's voice was pleading, "Honey, I know you're gonna be busy on your wedding trip, but do you think you could take a little time out to speak to us?"

"I'm not sure I understand. What is it you want me to speak about?"

Mavis clucked admiringly. "You city girls are so humble. Now what else would I be wanting you to teach us? About colors, of course. Ain't nobody got a fashion sense for color like you."

Rosa couldn't resist nudging Seth, whose jaw fell slack upon hearing Mavis's request. "Mercy, He was quick to answer that one," she whispered with a smug grin.

A delighted giggle erupted from Elise. "I. . .I'd be happy

to, Mavis."

Mavis sighed her relief. "Oh, thank you, honey." She placed a piece of paper in Elise's hand. "This here's my address. Give me a holler when you can." She hugged Elise quickly before disappearing into the guests.

Tanner smiled tenderly at his bride and planted a quick kiss on her forehead before grasping her hand and starting through the throng of well-wishers toward the front door. The crowd moved outside to the porch and continued to cheer as the newlyweds loaded into the buggy and headed toward Fort Worth.

Rosa stood at the porch railing and watched as the buggy disappeared down the road. She wiped a tear from her cheek. "God bless them," she whispered.

Becky wagged her tail and barked.

Seth smiled. "I believe He already has."

A Letter To Our Readers

Dear Reader:

In order that we might better contribute to your reading enjoyment, we would appreciate your taking a few minutes to respond to the following questions. When completed, please return to the following:

Rebecca Germany, Managing Editor
Heartsong Presents
P.O. Box 719
Uhrichsville, Ohio 44683

1. Did you enjoy reading *Her Father's Love*?
   - ❏ Very much. I would like to see more books by this author!
   - ❏ Moderately
     I would have enjoyed it more if _____

     _____

2. Are you a member of **Heartsong Presents**? ❏Yes ❏No
   If no, where did you purchase this book? _____

   _____

3. What influenced your decision to purchase this book? (Check those that apply.)

❏ Cover	❏ Back cover copy
❏ Title	❏ Friends
❏ Publicity	❏ Other_____

4. How would you rate, on a scale from 1 (poor) to 5 (superior), the cover design? _____

5. On a scale from 1 (poor) to 10 (superior), please rate the following elements.

___Heroine   ___Plot

___Hero   ___Inspirational theme

___Setting   ___Secondary characters

6. What settings would you like to see covered in **Heartsong Presents** books?_____

_____

_____

7. What are some inspirational themes you would like to see treated in future books?_____

_____

_____

8. Would you be interested in reading other **Heartsong Presents** titles?   ❏ Yes   ❏ No

9. Please check your age range:
   ❏ Under 18   ❏ 18-24   ❏ 25-34
   ❏ 35-45   ❏ 46-55   ❏ Over 55

10. How many hours per week do you read? _____.

Name _____

Occupation_____

Address_____

City_____ State_____ Zip _____